Irish author **Abby Green** ended a very glamorous career in film and TV—which really consisted of a lot of standing in the rain outside actors' trailers—to pursue her love of romance. After she'd bombarded Mills & Boon with manuscripts they kindly accepted one, and an author was born. She lives in Dublin, Ireland, and loves any excuse for distraction. Visit abby-green.com or email abbygreenauthor@gmail.com.

REDEEMED
BY HIS
STOLEN BRIDE

ABBY GREEN

MILLS & BOON

First Published in Great Britain 2019
by Mills & Boon, an imprint of HarperCollins*Publishers*
1 London Bridge Street, London, SE1 9GF

ISBN: 978-0-263-08666-9

MIX
Paper from
responsible sources
FSC® C007454

This book is produced from independently certified FSC™ paper
to ensure responsible forest management.
For more information visit www.harpercollins.co.uk/green.

Printed and bound in Great Britain
by CPI Group (UK) Ltd, Croydon, CR0 4YY

This is for Heidi Rice, who came up with
the idea of giving the jilted fiancée from
Confessions of a Pregnant Cinderella her own story. X

CHAPTER ONE

LEONORA FLORES DE LA VEGA couldn't seem to take her eyes off the man standing at the back of the crowd in the glittering ballroom. He towered over everyone around him, putting him at well over six feet.

He was also scowling, which only made his hawkish good looks even more forbidding and intimidating. And even from here Leonora was aware of his sheer masculine magnetism. As if there was an invisible thread tugging her attention to him whether she liked it or not.

She knew who Gabriel Ortega Cruz y Torres was. Everyone did. He came from one of Spain's most noble and oldest families. They owned huge swathes of the country and generated an income from banking, vineyards and real estate—just to name a few enterprises.

He was an intensely private man, but even so he had a reputation for being as ruthless in the bedroom as he was in business. Single, he was considered one of the most eligible bachelors in Europe, if not the world. But he appeared to be in no hurry to settle down. And when he did it would be with an undeniably well-connected woman who breathed the same rarefied air as he did.

And why should that even concern her? Leonora chastised herself. She might come from a family almost as well-connected as Gabriel's, but there the similarity ended. Her family had lost their fortune, and had been subsisting on scraps and the funds from opening up their *castillo* just outside Madrid. It was an ignominious state of affairs. And one that was becoming increasingly unsustainable.

She had never spoken to Gabriel Torres and was never likely to. A man like him wouldn't lower himself to consort with someone from a family of very faded glory. But she'd always been aware of him. From the moment she'd first laid eyes on him when he'd been about twenty-one and she'd been twelve. She'd watched him play polo—that had been before her family had lost everything due to her father's gambling habit, a long-standing source of shame that had kept her parents from venturing out in public for years.

She hadn't been able to take her eyes off Gabriel that day. He'd been so vital. So alive. He and the horse had moved as one, with awesome athleticism and grace. But it had been the expression on his face that had caught her— so intense and focused.

She'd overheard one of the opposing team say, 'Hey, Torres, lighten up. It's just a friendly game.'

He'd said nothing, just glowered at the man. Leonora could remember feeling an ache near her heart, as if she'd wanted to soothe him somehow...make him smile.

Which was ridiculous.

She became aware of the hubbub in the ballroom. Of the hundreds of eyes looking at her. And suddenly she came out of her reverie and back into the present moment. A moment that was going to change her life for ever.

A spurt of panic clutched at her gut and she breathed through it.

She was doing this for her family. For Matías. She had no choice. She was their only hope of redemption.

A light sweat broke out on her palms as she forced her gaze away from the man at the back of the room and found the man she *should* be looking at. Her fiancé. Lazaro Sanchez. He was devilishly handsome, with overlong dark blond hair and mesmerisingly unusual green eyes. Tall. He was almost as tall as—

She shook her head briefly. *No.* She had to stop thinking about him. She was about to become engaged to *this* man. This man she hardly knew, if she was honest. They'd had some dates. She didn't feel anything when she looked at him. Not like...*him*.

But Lazaro was kind and respectful. And, more importantly, he was prepared to bail her family out of their quagmire of debts and in so doing restore their respectability and secure Matías's future. In return... Well, Leonora was cynical enough to recognise ruthless ambition when she saw it. Lazaro Sanchez wanted to marry her in order to achieve a level of acceptance into the world she inhabited. Her only currency now was as a trophy to someone like him and she had no choice but to accept it.

She noticed then that Lazaro had a glowering expression on his face, not unlike the one on Gabriel Torres's. Something about that caught in Leonora's mind, but before she could unpick what it meant she realised that one of Lazaro's staff was making a motion, as if to say, *It's time.*

She tried to get his attention, 'Lazaro?'

He looked at her. Still glowering.

'Are you all right?' she asked. 'You look very fierce.'

His expression cleared. He held out a hand and she slipped hers into his. *Nothing.* No effect. She berated herself again. People in this world didn't marry for love or chemistry. They married strategically. Exactly as she was doing.

'Yes, fine...just a little preoccupied,' he said.

Unable to help herself, Leonora glanced back across the room, and this time Gabriel Torres's dark, compelling gaze met hers. A flash of heat went straight through her abdomen. Her fingers tightened reflexively around Lazaro's.

'Are *you* okay?' he asked her.

A surge of guilt blasted her. How could she be so compelled by another man when she was about to commit publicly to this one? She looked at Lazaro and forced a smile. 'Yes, I'm fine.'

His hand tightened around hers. 'I'm glad you have agreed to marry me, Leonora. I think we can have a good marriage, I think we can be…happy.'

Did he?

A semi-hysterical bubble rose up inside her. She had a sense of the massive room closing in around her, suffocating her. Lazaro let go of her hand and slipped his arm around her waist. The feeling of claustrophobia got worse.

His hand tightened on her waist, almost painfully, and Leonora hissed at him. *'Lazaro—'*

He looked at her with a strange expression on his face, his eyes burning.

'You're hurting me.'

Immediately he released his grip. 'I'm sorry.'

Leonora forced a smile. The sooner they got this announcement over with, the sooner she could get out of this room and get some air. She resolutely forced herself to keep her eyes averted from where Gabriel Torres stood, towering over everyone else around him. Powerful. Magnetic. Disturbing.

A waiter approached with champagne and she took two glasses, handing one to Lazaro. She saw movement nearby and said, 'Your advisors are making motions that it's time to make the announcement. Ready?'

Lazaro looked at her, and she clung to the resolve she could see in his eyes.

He clinked his glass to hers. 'Yes, let's do it.'

He put his arm around her waist again and Leonora forced a smile through the lingering claustrophobia. He started speaking, but she didn't really take in his words, letting them roll over her.

Against every effort, her eye was drawn back across the crowd to where Gabriel Torres stood. He was still watching her, with a disconcertingly intense gaze. Leonora started to tremble lightly under the force of it.

Suddenly a voice rang out. *'Wait! Stop!'*

It shook Leonora out of her trance. It was a woman, who'd pushed through the crowd near the dais. She was being held back by security guards. She was dressed like the wait staff, in a white shirt and black skirt. Vibrant red hair, up in a bun. She was very pretty. Bright blue eyes.

She was looking at Lazaro, and then she said, 'You need to know something. I'm pregnant. With your child.'

For long seconds time was suspended, and then everything seemed to go into slow motion as Leonora felt Lazaro's arm leave her waist. She watched as the woman said something else, not hearing what it was through the buzzing in her head.

Lazaro stepped down off the dais to talk to the woman, holding her arm. She looked very petite next to him. Vaguely, ridiculously, Leonora appreciated that they looked good together.

She couldn't hear what they were saying, and then the woman was being led away.

Lazaro turned back to look at her, his expression veering between shock, anger and contrition.

He came back up on to the dais and said something to the crowd—she wasn't sure what. Too many feelings were rolling over her—chief of which, she was ashamed to admit, was a sense of relief. But that was quickly eclipsed when she looked around and saw the crowd whispering. Some people were looking at her with pity and others with something far less benign. A malicious glee at the fall of one of their own.

She'd tried to buy her way out of debt and shame and now she felt as exposed as if she were naked. And *he* was still there. At the back. Looking at her with a grim expression.

She turned away and saw Lazaro. She backed away and then she stopped. Maybe this was just some hideous case of mistaken identity.

'Is it true?'

But Lazaro said nothing, and his silence said everything. He looked guilty.

He held out a hand. 'Leonora, please…let me explain.'

It was real.

She became aware of the burn of humiliation. She shook her head. 'I can't agree to marry you. Not now.'

She sent up a silent *thank you* that her parents weren't there to witness this moment. Or Matías. He would see that she was upset and that would upset him.

She cast a look around, instinctively seeking an escape route. All she saw were judgemental eyes. Mocking eyes.

She looked at Lazaro for one last time, dismay and humiliation scoring her insides like a knife. 'How could you do this to me? In front of all these people?'

Without waiting for a response, she put her glass down on the nearest surface and turned and fled, making for the nearest exit with no clue where to go.

The first thing she saw was a Ladies' sign, and she followed it to the bathroom, which was mercifully empty. She locked herself into a stall and sat down on the closed toilet.

She was trembling, her heart pounding. She forced herself to take deep breaths, and just as she was starting to feel marginally calmer the door opened. It sounded as if at least three women were coming in, all chattering. About her and Lazaro.

'Who'd marry her now? She's so desperate she was willing to marry some nouveau riche billionaire...'

'Where did Sanchez even come from?'

'Some say he grew up on the streets.'

'The de la Vegas can't survive this. All they have is her and that brother of hers, who everyone knows is a—'

At the mention of Leonora's beloved brother she opened the door and stepped out of the stall, coming face-to-face with the three gossipers. The chatter stopped instantly.

One blanched, one went red, but the other one was totally unrepentant. Leonora was too upset to speak. She just watched as they collected their things and walked out in silence, taking no sense of satisfaction in having routed them because she knew they'd only start gossiping again as soon as they were out of earshot.

She went over to the sink and put her hands on the counter, looking at herself in the mirror but only vaguely registering that her outward appearance—relatively calm—belied the storm inside. She could only give thanks that the women hadn't witnessed her falling apart.

She took a deep breath and ran some cold water over her hands and wrists. She hoped that by the time she emerged there would be no one else waiting to witness her walk of shame.

At that instant a face popped into her head. *Gabriel Torres.* His hawk-like features were as vivid as if he were standing in front of her. She went hot and then cold at the thought of *him* having witnessed her public humiliation.

But she wouldn't see him again. Because she wouldn't be emerging in public for a long time.

She took a breath and steeled herself before heading back out and into the lobby, hoping for a discreet getaway.

* * *

Where was she?

Gabriel Torres looked left and right outside the function room, but there was no sign of the dark-haired woman in the long strapless red dress. The dress that clung to her elegant curves in a way that had made his blood pound for the first time in a long time. The compulsion to follow her prickled over his skin now; he wasn't someone normally given to such impetuosity.

He had only come here this evening to see for himself what Lazaro Sanchez was up to, because he didn't trust the man as far as he could throw him. Especially when everything he did seemed to be designed personally to get under Gabriel's skin. And because they were both involved in a very competitive and lucrative bid for a public project.

Recently Sanchez had even gone so far as to concoct a story that he and Gabriel were half-brothers. He'd accosted Gabriel at an event they'd both attended and when Gabriel had tried to walk away, disgusted at the insinuation that they could be related, Sanchez had stopped him, telling him of a day, many years before, when he had confronted Gabriel's father, claiming to be his son.

To Gabriel's surprise and shock he'd remembered the incident—and the skinny kid who had been waiting for them outside a restaurant in central Madrid. It had been his birthday—one of the very rare occasions when his dysfunctional family had put on a united front.

Gabriel had never been naïve about either of his parents. It was quite possible that his serially philandering father might have sired a bastard along the way. For a family like the Cruz y Torres, whose vast dynasty stretched back to the Middle Ages, such occurrences by opportunists were frequent and, frankly, to be expected.

So, for all he knew, Sanchez could be his brother but

he suspected it was more likely to be a ruse to get under Gabriel's skin.

Ironically enough, Gabriel's father was at this event too, this evening, but Gabriel had ignored him. They barely tolerated each other at the best of times, and he'd had no doubt that the only reason his father had been there was probably the free-flowing booze or a woman.

Since Sanchez's claim to be related to Gabriel, he'd been kept at a certain distance. But tonight had been one of his most audacious moves yet: announcing his engagement to one of Spain's most well-connected women, whose own family rivalled Gabriel's in lineage and legacy.

Marriage to someone like Leonora Flores de la Vega would elevate Sanchez to a place that would make it that much harder to ignore him. Gabriel had to hand it to him for sheer chutzpah.

Clearly he hadn't been intending on marrying Leonora Flores for her money—her family were famously broke after her father's well-documented gambling problems. Her worth came in her name and lineage.

Gabriel had heard the whispers in the crowd. Whispers that Sanchez had offered her a deal—he'd pay off her family debts and in return buy his way into the world he was so desperate to be a part of that he claimed to be Gabriel's blood relation.

Gabriel didn't know Leonora personally, but he knew *of* her, and their paths had crossed over the years at social events. But coming here this evening, seeing her standing up on that dais beside Sanchez, had reminded him that there was something about her that had always snagged his attention. He'd noticed it again this evening. Enough to distract him from Lazaro Sanchez.

Her beautiful face had been composed. Revealing nothing. Her long dark hair pulled back and sleek, showing off the exquisite bone structure of her face. Wide almond-shaped eyes. Dark lashes. A full mouth that hinted at a level of sensuality Gabriel sensed she wasn't entirely comfortable with.

He'd racked his brains to think of the last time he'd seen her. It hadn't been recent. She'd grown up in the meantime. Now she was a woman—and a stunningly beautiful woman at that.

Gabriel had found himself staring at her, willing her to look at him, *needing* her to look at him. And then she had. He'd felt the impact of that contact from across the room. An instantaneous jolt of sexual awareness surging through his blood.

She'd kept on looking at Gabriel and he'd seen the flicker of panic in her eyes. Along with something else far more potent.

She wanted him.

That awareness, together with seeing Sanchez's arm around her waist, had caught at something unexpected inside Gabriel. Something hot and visceral. A sense of... possessiveness.

When Sanchez had announced their engagement, Gabriel had felt an inexplicable and almost overwhelming urge to disrupt proceedings, but just at that moment another voice had rung out. A voice coming from the petite red-haired woman near the dais, claiming to be pregnant with Sanchez's child.

Leonora had fled, and Gabriel had watched her go, knowing immediately that he would go after her. He'd never felt such a primal pull towards anyone.

He'd looked at Sanchez and the animosity he'd felt towards the man had compelled him to mock him for his abortive attempt to buy respectability and for bringing his domestic dramas into the public domain.

But all thoughts of Sanchez were gone now, as he looked left and right for Leonora Flores.

She was gone.

An alien sensation stopped Gabriel in his tracks and he realised it was the sensation of something having slipped through his fingers.

For a man who generally obtained his every want and desire, it was unwelcome. And an unpleasant reminder that he was acting out of character. Pursuing a woman when he didn't need to. If he wanted a woman that badly he could walk back into the room behind him and take his pick. But a new restlessness prickled under his skin. He didn't want one of *them*. So eager, so desperate. He wanted *her*.

And then, as if answering his silent call, he saw her, standing behind the elaborate foliage screening the lobby and entrance from the rest of the hotel. He saw what she saw: a bank of waiting paparazzi outside the main door of the hotel, and no other means of escape.

There was no way he was going to let her out of his sight again. And if the opportunity presented itself to re-mind Sanchez of where he belonged, Gabriel would be a fool not to exploit it.

Leonora cursed silently. Between the fronds of the exotic plant she could see where the photographers were lined up, no doubt ready to capture the smiling couple emerging from the hotel. There was no other way out without going through the lobby. One way or another they would see her, either scuttling away as if she was the one in the wrong, or walking out without her new fiancé.

Just as she was steeling herself to run the gauntlet, she felt the back of her neck prickle with awareness and her skin tingled all over.

She turned around and Gabriel Ortega Cruz y Torres was

standing a couple of feet away, looking at her. She gulped. He was even taller up close. Broader. Thick dark hair swept back off his forehead. Deep-set dark eyes. Strong brows. A patrician nose and a firm, unyielding mouth.

His bottom lip was surprisingly lush, though, softening the hard edges of his face and making her wonder what it would feel like to touch...kiss... She could imagine him lounging on jewel-coloured cushions, summoning his minions.

Summoning his lovers.

A wave of heat flashed through her body. She was losing it. She *never* imagined kissing men. She was a twenty-four-year-old virgin, because her life had revolved around her parents, the castle and her disabled brother. She'd been more of a mother than a sister to her brother, since their world had imploded after her father's gambling excesses. She'd literally had no time for anything else. Anything normal. Like relationships.

Before she could even think of something to say Gabriel came forward and his scent reached her nostrils, sharp and infinitely masculine. Exotic.

'Would you like me to get you out of here?'

His voice was deep and compelling.

Leonora's response was swift and instinctive. She nodded.

'We'll go out through the main entrance. Don't look left or right, just let me guide you.'

He plucked something out of his pocket and Leonora saw that it was a phone. He issued a curt instruction and put the phone back, his eyes never leaving hers.

'My car is outside. Let's go.'

Before Leonora knew what was happening Gabriel Torres had taken her elbow in his hand and they were already halfway across the lobby. Flashes erupted from outside, and as soon as they got through the doors there was a barrage of noise and calls.

'Leonora! Where's Lazaro Sanchez?'

Leonora ignored it all and followed Gabriel's instructions, looking straight ahead.

A sleek low-slung silver bullet of a car was parked by the kerb and the doorman sprang aside as Gabriel helped her into the front passenger seat. The door was shut, cocooning her in expensive leather and metal and blissful silence, which was only broken briefly when Gabriel came around to the driver's side and opened the door, settling himself into the car.

Within seconds they were moving through the throng of press, who had to part to let them through. Leonora flinched at the bright flashes from their cameras as the paparazzi pressed cameras up to the window to get their shots.

'I should have tried to leave through a back entrance. I'll be on every front page tomorrow.'

She felt Gabriel glance at her. 'Why should you? You've nothing to be ashamed of.'

Leonora's heart was pounding. She saw Gabriel's hand work the gearstick. Square-shaped long fingers. Short, blunt nails. Masculine.

Her lower body clenched.

'You didn't have to do this,' she said.

Her voice was husky. She looked at Gabriel, whose jaw was tight.

'It's nothing. You shouldn't have been thrown to the wolves like that.'

She got the impression that he was angry. On her behalf. She barely knew him. Her relief at being out of that situation was taking the edges off her own anger at Lazaro.

'Well…thank you.'

She noticed then that they were driving through one of

Madrid's exclusive city enclaves. Leafy streets and chic cosmopolitan bars and restaurants. Expensive antique shops and designer boutiques. Elegant buildings mixed with new architecture.

Feeling embarrassed now, and thinking that Gabriel might be regretting his good deed, Leonora said, 'You really don't have to take me home. I'm the other way, anyway. I can jump out here and get a taxi.'

He shook his head and glanced in the rear-view mirror. 'Not if you don't want them to follow you home, you can't.'

Leonora looked behind them and saw a couple of motorbikes weaving in and out of traffic, following them. Her heart sank at the thought of them outside the family estate. If Matías saw them he'd get confused and upset...

At that moment Gabriel said, 'Hang on,' and then surged ahead as a traffic light turned to red. He negotiated a couple of rapid turns down dark side streets that had Leonora's heart jumping into her throat, but at no point did she feel unsafe. It was exhilarating.

With the next turn into a quiet residential street Leonora sucked in a breath. It looked as if they were going to drive straight into a wall, but it quickly revealed itself to be a door that opened and allowed them entry down into a private garage under the building.

Gabriel pulled to a stop beside a row of equally sleek cars. 'I think we lost them at the last traffic lights.'

Silence descended around them. 'Where are we?' she asked.

'At my city apartment. You can wait here for a bit—let them lose you. I'll organise for you to get home later. If you want.'

If you want.

Leonora looked at Gabriel, still reeling at everything that had happened and at the fact that he was her rescuer.

His eyes were on her, dark and unreadable, and yet she felt as if some silent communication was taking place. Something she didn't understand fully. Or didn't want to investigate fully.

'Okay…if you're sure. I don't want to bother you.'

He shook his head. 'You're not bothering me. Don't worry.'

He undid his seat-belt and uncoiled his tall frame from the car. He came around and opened her door and held out a hand.

Leonora almost didn't want to touch him, afraid of how she'd react. She could still feel the imprint of his hand on her elbow. But she couldn't dither, so she put her hand in his and let him pull her out. And she'd been right to be afraid, because a jolt of electricity ran up her arm and right down into her core.

By the time she straightened up she was breathless. And she was so close to Gabriel that one more step would bring her flush with his body. She could sense the whipcord strength beneath his bespoke suit. Her eye line rested just below his bowtie.

His hand wrapped around hers. 'Okay?'

She looked up and forced a smile, trying not to be intimidated by the sheer masculine beauty of the man. His proximity. 'Fine… Just a bit shaky after the paparazzi. Normally I don't register on their radar.'

Not the way this man did. He was slavishly followed and speculated upon by press eager to get a story on the reclusive billionaire. She thought of the papers tomorrow. Her head hurt at the prospect of her parents' reaction. They were depending on her to redeem the family name and finances, not to embroil them in another scandal.

Gabriel let her hand go and Leonora suddenly realised something with dismay. 'My bag and coat!'

Lazaro had arranged for someone to take them to the cloakroom at the hotel.

Gabriel said, 'Come upstairs and I'll arrange for them to be delivered here.'

He opened a door that led out into a dimly lit foyer. A security guard stepped into the light. 'Good evening, Señor Torres.'

'Good evening, Pancho. One of my team will be delivering something shortly. Let them in and send it up, please.'

'Of course, sir.'

Gabriel put his hand on Leonora's back, guiding her with a barely perceptible touch over to an elevator. Even so, she could feel his hand through her dress, and had the ridiculous urge to sink back against him, let him take her weight.

It unnerved her how much he made her *feel*, so she stood apart from him in the small space as the doors slid shut and he pressed a button. It rose silently and stopped a few seconds later with a small jerking motion.

The doors slid open and Gabriel put out a hand, indicating for Leonora to precede him. She stepped out and into a stunning penthouse apartment. It had all the original features of the building's era—around the nineteenth century, Leonora guessed—but none of the fussiness.

It was a very contemporary apartment in the shell of one of Madrid's classic buildings. Modern art hung on the walls, with spotlights directing the eye to bold slashing strokes and colours. Surprisingly sensual. Something about the design—the lack of clutter, the open spaces—soothed her. The furniture was deceptively plain and unobtrusive, letting the interior speak for itself. She'd never seen anything quite like it.

She watched as Gabriel strode over to French doors, opening them to let some air in. Leonora only realised then how close it was. The late-summer city heat was still oppressive. He took his phone out of his pocket and made a call, speaking in low tones. She assumed he was arranging to have her things collected.

He turned around to face her then, tugging at his bowtie, undoing it. Opening the top button of his shirt. She almost looked away, feeling as if she was intruding on some intimacy.

He gestured with a hand to a couch. 'Please—sit, make yourself comfortable...'

Leonora stepped further into the room, feeling naked without her wrap or bag. 'I'm fine, thank you. You have a beautiful apartment.'

No doubt it was just one of the hundreds of properties owned by him and his family all over Spain and the world.

It was well known that he was seen very much as the patriarch of his family, even though his father was still alive. And Leonora was vaguely aware of a rumour about his younger sister going off the rails and how she'd been sent abroad to clean up her act.

She shivered slightly at the thought of what it must be like to face a disapproving or angry Gabriel Torres. She didn't even know his sister, or if the rumour was true, but she already felt sorry for her.

'Would you like a drink?' He walked over to an elaborate drinks cabinet. 'I have whiskey, brandy, champagne, wine, gin—'

'I'll have a little whiskey please,' she blurted out, needing something to settle her clanging nerves.

He poured dark golden liquid into a small tumbler and brought it over to her. 'It's Irish. I believe it's meant to be very good.'

Leonora took it, distracted by the bowtie dangling at his

neck and the open top button of his shirt. She could see dark bronzed skin. A hint of hair.

'You haven't tasted it?'

He shook his head. 'I don't drink.'

She watched as he moved back, giving her space. It fitted that he didn't drink. He seemed far too controlled. Exacting. Alert. She wondered why he didn't, but wasn't going to ask.

As if he could read her mind, though, he supplied, 'I was put off after watching how alcohol affected people's judgement and their decision-making. Not least my father's. He almost ruined the family business.'

So that was why Gabriel now ran their extensive operation.

'I'm sorry to hear that…' Impulsively she added, 'I have some idea of what you're talking about.'

She wondered why she'd said that, but there was something about being in this space with this man that didn't feel entirely real.

To her relief he didn't say anything, or ask her to elaborate on the fact that her father's vices had driven them to the brink and over. Anyway, he probably knew the sordid details. Most people did. But for the first time she didn't feel that burning rise of shame. Maybe it was his admission that his family wasn't perfect either.

He said, 'I'm sorry for what happened to you this evening. You didn't deserve that. You're too good for a man like Lazaro Sanchez.'

Leonora clutched the tumbler to her chest. She'd yet to take a sip of the drink. 'You don't have to be sorry. It wasn't your fault. And how can you say I'm too good for him? You don't even know me.'

'Don't I?' he asked softly, raising a dark brow. 'We come from the same world, Leonora. We might not have had a conversation before now, but we know more about each other than you realise—and I'm not talking about idle gossip. I'm talking about the lives we've led. The expectations on our shoulders. The life built on legacy and duty. Responsibility.'

CHAPTER TWO

GABRIEL MARVELLED AT how expressive Leonora was. She clearly hadn't expected him to say that. He'd caught her unawares. Her eyes were wide on his, as if he'd shocked her.

He realised now that they weren't dark brown, as he'd assumed. They were grey. Like a stormy ocean. But even as he had that fanciful notion she seemed to come back to herself and her face resumed its serene mask. The same one she'd been wearing earlier, standing beside Lazaro Sanchez. Before all hell had broken loose.

She took a sip of her drink and he noticed her hand wasn't entirely steady. He had to clench his fist to stop from reaching out and taking her hand in his. He saw her throat work as she swallowed and he imagined the burn of the alcohol as it slipped down into her stomach, radiating heat. Mirroring the heat he felt in his blood.

Dios, but she was stunning. Possibly the most beautiful woman he'd ever seen. And she was getting to him in a way that made him distinctly uncomfortable. Usually when he desired a woman it was a manageable thing. Right now it was taking all his restraint not to seduce Leonora to within an inch of her life and demand the satisfaction his body was crying out for. A kind of satisfaction that he knew instinctively would eclipse anything he'd ever experienced before.

He stepped back and gestured to a nearby couch. 'Please, sit down. Your things should be here soon.'

* * *

For a long moment Leonora couldn't move. She was still in shock at how succinctly Gabriel had summed up her existence.

'The lives we've led... The expectations on our shoulders... The life built on legacy and duty. Responsibility.'

She'd never felt that anyone could possibly understand what her life was like. She had very little to complain about and yet sometimes she felt as trapped as if she was in jail.

He was looking at her. He'd just asked if she wanted to sit down.

She shook her head jerkily. 'No, I'm fine. Thank you.'

She felt restless, and she walked over to where floor-to-ceiling windows looked out over a terrace and further, to the skyline of Madrid under a clear starlit sky. She had a very fleeting moment of wondering what Lazaro was doing right now. Dealing with the mother of his child?

A tiny sense of hysteria at what had happened rose up and she took another hasty sip of whiskey to try and force it back down.

Gabriel came to stand near her. She could see him in the reflection of the window. He'd taken off his jacket and his chest and shoulders looked impossibly broad under the snowy shirt.

She saw her own reflection. The strapless red dress. She'd hoped its elegant simplicity would prove to be timeless, because it was many seasons out of date. She saw the glittering drop earrings hanging from her earlobes that looked like diamonds. But they weren't diamonds at all. They were cubic zirconia. It was a long time since she'd worn any real family jewels. They'd all been sold by her father to get money for gambling.

She felt like a fraud, and the humiliation from earlier

rose up again. She quickly downed the last of her drink, guiltily relishing the last dregs of comfort from the alcohol.

She turned to face Gabriel, avoiding his eye. 'I should leave—go home. My mother and father will be worried.'

And Matías.

Just thinking of him made her heart hurt. What would happen to them now? If they lost the castle then that was it. They would have hit rock bottom with no way back. An entire dynasty and legacy wiped out through the actions of her father...

'Don't go yet.'

She looked at Gabriel. Her heart thumped hard. His face was all lean angles and harsh lines. And then softened by that ridiculously sensual mouth.

'We're still waiting for your things.'

Leonora was torn. She wanted to appear totally at ease and sophisticated, draping herself artfully on one of the sofas while wittily regaling Gabriel with inconsequential chatter. But that wasn't her. Had never been her.

'I can get them tomorrow. They're not that important.'

She felt that the longer she stood there the quicker he'd see that he was having an effect on her.

He came closer and moved to take the empty glass from her hand. He put his fingers over hers. A deliberate move? The breath stuck in her throat. He was so...*vital*. Lazaro had never had this effect on her and she'd believed that it would make for a better marriage. No extreme feelings or wants.

Gabriel said, 'The paparazzi will know for sure by now that your engagement wasn't announced. They'll be actively hunting you down. Waiting for you. You should call your parents—warn them to stay inside.'

Leonora swallowed. Gabriel's fingers were still on hers. 'But I can't just...stay here.'

'Of course you can.' He took the glass out of her nerveless fingers and in the same motion, with his other hand, he handed her his phone. 'Use this.'

It seemed to be a foregone conclusion. And she knew he was right. She couldn't go back home now and face a barrage of lights and questions. Out of concern for Matías as much as anything else.

Leonora moved away from Gabriel and dialled her home number. Her mother answered, immediately concerned, and Leonora rushed to assure her that everything was okay. She filled her in on the broad strokes of what had happened and told her not to worry. She told her that she'd spend the night elsewhere, to draw the press away from the de la Vega home. Her mother sounded disappointed—and then just weary. They'd been here before, with the press camped outside.

When she'd ended the conversation, after checking that Matías was okay, Leonora handed the phone back.

Gabriel said, 'Your brother is not well?'

Leonora gave a small tight smile. 'He has...learning difficulties. Since birth. He's home at the moment—from the school he attends just outside Madrid.'

The school that was paid for out of the receipts from tours around the Flores de la Vega castle. And with the money from the designer clothes and jewellery Leonora sold over the years online. The school that he loved and thrived in. The school that was offering him a real chance at a life in the outside world as he moved into adulthood.

The school that they would no longer be able to afford if they had to sell the castle—the only thing keeping them afloat in a sea of debts.

'He picks up on moods and tension very acutely, so he'd be upset if he knew the press were outside, or if there was anything wrong with me.'

'You're close?'

Leonora looked at Gabriel, expecting to see the same look most people had when they heard about Matías, varying between mild disdain and salacious curiosity. Or pity. But Gabriel's face and eyes held none of those things. Just a genuine question.

She nodded, feeling emotional. 'The closest. He's eighteen now, and when he was born I was six. He was like my baby more than my little brother.'

'That would have been before your fortunes…changed.'

Leonora appreciated his attempt at tact. He was obviously referring to the fact that her parents had once been such fixtures on the Spanish social scene that they probably hadn't been around much to parent. Making their fall from grace even more explosive. They'd gone down in a ball of flames and infamy when her father had been thrown out of the casino in Monte Carlo with his wife clinging to his coat, weeping uncontrollably.

That was one of the reasons for their reclusiveness these days. Her parents' shame. Hence their desire and need for redemption. Through Leonora.

She diverted her mind from that and said, 'Something like that. Yes.' She looked away, embarrassed.

'That was them—not you. You're not like them.'

Leonora looked at him. Had he moved closer? The way he made her feel—the way he seemed to be looking deeper into her than anyone else ever had—made her prickly.

'You don't know that I don't have a gambling habit.'

He seemed to consider this for a moment, and then he said, 'True, I don't. But I don't believe you do.'

He was definitely closer now. Close enough for Leonora to see the stubble lining his jaw. And that his eyes had golden flecks—they weren't just brown.

She shook her head. 'Why are you doing this? Why do

you care what happens to me? We've never met before this evening. I mean…not properly.'

Even with Leonora's family connections they'd moved in a lesser sphere than the Torres family.

'No. But our paths have crossed—even if just peripherally. I realised something this evening—I have always noticed you…on the edges. As if you'd prefer to disappear.'

Leonora blushed to think she'd been so transparent.

'And I realised something else.'

She looked at him.

'You have become a very beautiful woman.'

A tingling rush of heat coursed through her blood. The way he was looking at her was so…*intense*. She could almost feel it…as if he was touching her.

He took another step closer. Almost close enough now that she could imagine him bending down and pressing his mouth to hers.

Leonora was barely breathing. She was hot—so hot. All over. Deep down where no man had ever had any effect on her before.

'I want you, Leonora.'

For a long, suspended moment neither one of them moved. Gabriel was watching her as she struggled to absorb this information. So, all these sensations making her melt from the inside out…it wasn't just her.

For a second it was too heady to consider. The fact that he thought she was beautiful. And that he wanted her. *Her*. A woman who lived a more sheltered existence than most nuns.

At that moment there was a chiming sound. Gabriel emitted a curse under his breath and said, 'Don't move. That's the concierge with your things.'

He turned and she watched him walk across the vast room with athletic grace. He disappeared and she heard a door open, low voices. She saw the French doors and suddenly needed—craved—oxygen. She walked outside, drawing in deep lungsful of the night air. The sounds of traffic floating up from nearby streets helped to ground her in reality a little.

What was she doing? Practically falling into Gabriel Torres's arms after mere words? He was probably just being polite, helping to soothe what he assumed was her damaged ego. But in all honesty relief was her overriding feeling when she thought about Lazaro and the wreckage of their engagement.

It had been an audacious plan in any case—agreeing to marry a man purely for strategic reasons. Because it would benefit them both. It shamed her now. Yet she knew it was silly to feel shame, because her parents' marriage had been a strategic one. In their world *every* marriage was a strategic one. Too much was at stake when legacies and dynasties had to be passed down to the next generation for emotion to be involved in making a marriage.

The fact that her parents got on and had some affection for each other was just a bonus. It had helped them weather the storm of infamy and their son's vulnerabilities.

But Leonora—much to her eternal embarrassment—had always secretly harboured a desire for more. For a *real* relationship. For love. Happiness. She saw visiting tourist couples walking through the castle and its grounds, sharing kisses, holding hands. Whispering things to each other.

She'd met an old English couple, married for fifty years. They'd exuded such an aura of contentment and happiness. She knew what they had was rare, but not unobtainable. For normal people. Not for her.

When Lazaro Sanchez had shown an interest and taken her on a few dates, and when he'd put forward his proposal and the fact that he was offering to pull them out of their quagmire of debts, Leonora had known that she had no choice. She had responsibilities, just as Gabriel had said. The Flores de la Vega legacy was bigger than her secret hopes and dreams for a different life. A more fulfilled life.

'I want you, Leonora.'

She shivered, even though it wasn't cold. She shivered with awareness. With desire.

'I have always noticed you...on the edges. As if you'd prefer to disappear.'

How could a man who was little more than a stranger— no matter how much their worlds might have collided over the years—*get* her? More than anyone had ever got her before?

She'd never felt seen in her life. She'd hovered on the edges, exactly as he'd described. Out of the innate shyness that she had to work hard to overcome. Out of her concern for Matías, who found social situations very challenging.

And also because she'd never really enjoyed the social scene of their world. It had always reminded her of a medieval royal court, with its intrigue and politics. Petty cruelties. The way so-called friends had treated her and her parents and her brother like pariahs ever since they'd become *persona non grata* had been a formative lesson in human nature.

Had Gabriel Torres really told her that he wanted her? So bold? So direct?

Yes. He was that kind of man. He would just say what he wanted and expect results.

Leonora looked out over the city stretching before her. Millions of people living their lives. Millions of possibilities.

It was as if she'd stepped out of her life and into an alternative realm. Where anything could happen. She was in a moment out of time. In a place she'd never expected to be. With a man she would never in a million years have expected to know her name. Let alone...*desire* her.

Unless it wasn't desire.

It must be pity.

A wave of humiliation rose up through her. Oh, God, was she so desperate that she really believed—?

She heard a noise and tensed to face Gabriel again. She needed to leave. *Now.*

Gabriel saw the moment Leonora heard him return. Her slim shoulders were suddenly a tense line. He stood behind her, drinking in her graceful figure. The smooth pale olive skin of her back. The sleek dark ponytail that he wanted to wrap around his fist so he could tilt her head back, giving him access to her lush mouth.

He might have started this evening fixated on Lazaro Sanchez, and wondering what the man was up to, but now all he could see was this woman.

'I have your things.'

She turned around but he noticed that she avoided his eye.

She held out a hand. 'Thank you. I really should go now. There's a back entrance into the estate. I can use that. I'm sure they won't see me.'

Gabriel handed her the wrap and bag, noting how she avoided touching his hand. A novelty when he was used to women throwing themselves at him. Especially if he told them that he wanted them.

'Are you really willing to take that risk?'

She put her wrap around her shoulders, covering up her skin, crossing it over her chest like a shawl.

Eventually she looked at him. 'Look, thank you for helping me, but you really don't need to go out of your way to do any more.'

Gabriel moved closer to her, watching how her eyes

flared and colour tinged her cheeks. She wanted him. He knew it.

'Did you not hear what I said?'

She swallowed. Her fingers clutched her wrap.

For a second the possibility trickled into Gabriel's mind that she was different from other women he knew in terms of experience, but he batted it away. She was twenty-four. To be inexperienced at her age, with her stunning beauty, in this modern cynical world, was practically an impossibility. Far more likely she was playing him. She knew he wanted her and she was getting off on watching him work to seduce her.

There was little novelty in Gabriel's world and he suspected it was the same for her. She was hardly a wide-eyed innocent when she'd been about to announce a business arrangement masquerading as a marriage.

'I want you, Leonora. You felt it too this evening. I saw it.'

She flushed and her eyes were huge. 'But…we don't even know each other. How can—?'

'How can it be possible?' Gabriel decided he'd indulge her faux innocence. 'Because chemistry transcends such mundanities.'

Every line in her body was tense.

'You don't have to do this, you know.'

There was a fierce pride in the aristocratic lines of her beautiful face. Her eyes had turned stormy.

'I don't need your pity, Gabriel.'

Leonora was resisting the pull she felt to this man with every atom of her being. He was toying with her. He had no clue how inexperienced she was and she wasn't about to let him expose her any more than she'd already been exposed tonight.

She went to move past him, intent on getting out of there

before she could unravel completely, but he caught her hand, stopping her. Heat travelled up her arm. She clenched her jaw.

'You seriously think I *pity* you?'

The incredulity in his tone compelled her to face him, her hand still in his. He was frowning. Suddenly she was very aware of their proximity, and of the darkness of his chest under the white shirt.

She swallowed. 'Maybe you just feel sorry for me...for what happened. You feel some kind of responsibility to make me feel...better.'

Even as she said this out loud she wanted to cringe. It sounded ridiculous.

He shook his head. 'You give me far too much credit. I'm not that nice. I told you I want you because I meant it. And I believe you want me too. You wanted me even as you stood beside your fiancé.'

Leonora flushed with guilty heat. She tried to pull her hand back but Gabriel didn't let go. He tugged her closer. She couldn't breathe.

'You don't believe I want you? I can prove to you that I do. And that you want me.'

Leonora knew that if she tugged hard she'd be free. She knew that if she did that, and if she turned and walked away, he wouldn't stop her. He was too proud for that. Too sophisticated to chase a woman or force her. And yet...she couldn't move. *Didn't want to.* That sense of being in a moment outside time, outside of her life, was acute.

As if sensing her vacillation, Gabriel said, 'Here you are beholden to no one. There's no duty or responsibility. We're just two people. A man and a woman who want each other. Who are free to indulge our mutual desire.'

Leonora searched the hard planes of his face, those dark eyes. Was it really that simple? Could it be that simple? *Was* she free?

She thought of where she would be now if that woman hadn't interrupted the announcement of her engagement.

She would be in a very similar situation with a man she'd liked, but hadn't wanted. Maybe he would be kissing her now and she would be feeling nothing, resigning herself to the fact that this was as good as it would get. Because so much more was at stake. The future of her family. Her brother's security.

She considered the vagaries of fate and timing and how she might not be here at all, how she wouldn't be feeling this terrifying but exhilarating wildness coursing through her blood right now.

But she was. And it sank in that Gabriel Torres was deadly serious. He wasn't being nice. Or pitying her. He wanted her. And she wanted him. For one night. One night out of time.

The wildness rushing through her body turned into something far more reckless. Tonight she really was free. Tomorrow she would return to reality and pick up the pieces of her life.

She wanted to seize this moment that fate had handed her. A chance to experience true desire with a man who wanted her for *her*. Not because of who she was or what her name represented.

Gabriel was watching her. Reading her.

Without saying a word, letting his actions speak for him, he let her hand go and reached for her wrap, tugging it out of her hands, pulling it off her shoulders slowly. The silk trailed across her skin and she shivered minutely at the sensation. She'd never thought of herself as sensual before, but she felt sensual now. Under his gaze.

His eyes not leaving hers, he draped the wrap over the back of a nearby chair and Leonora could see it out of the corner of her eyes, a vivid red splash of colour.

Danger. *Passion.*

He took her bag out of her hand and put it down. Anticipation built inside her, deep down. Coiling tight. She couldn't take her eyes off his face.

He said, 'I've told you I want you and I mean it. I haven't wanted a woman like this in a long time. But you owe me nothing. I brought you here to give you refuge, and my guest suite is at your disposal for as long as you need it. It's your choice what happens next.'

She let out the breath she'd been holding unconsciously. She hadn't expected that kind of consideration. And at that moment Leonora almost resented him for not just kissing her and taking the decision out of her hands.

She knew it would be so easy to gather up her wrap and bag and say, *No, sorry...not now.* But something inside her had bloomed into life and she suspected he knew that very well. Better than she did.

She felt totally out of her depth. Another woman, more experienced, would no doubt be sliding her arms around his neck, pressing herself against every hard muscle of his body. But she felt paralysed with sudden shyness.

Gabriel's gaze narrowed on her face. He frowned slightly. 'Leonora, if you don't want to—'

'I do,' she blurted out before she could lose her nerve. 'I do...want you.'

She stepped closer. They were almost touching. His sheer physicality was overwhelming but it didn't intimidate her. It excited her.

He put his hands on her arms and tugged her closer. She rested her palms on his chest. It was like steel. A spasm of sheer lust gripped her insides in a vice of tension. She pressed her thighs together to stem the heat flooding her core. But it was impossible. Every nerve quivered with anticipation and her heart was thumping so loudly she was sure it had to be audible.

Slowly, Gabriel took his hand off one of her arms and brought it up behind her head. She felt him undo her hair, so that it was loosened out of the ponytail. He massaged her scalp, his long fingers strong but surprisingly gentle. It made something else quiver inside her. Not just desire. *Emotion.*

But before that could really register he was lowering his head to hers, and as if in some desperate bid to cling on to a semblance of reality she kept her eyes on his, on those gold-flecked pools of brown. Intense and direct. Anchoring her to the moment.

But any hope of clinging to reality dissolved in a flash flood of heat when his mouth touched hers. Firm and unyielding. Soft but hard. Masterful. She was helpless against the giddy rush of desire that ripped through her body as his mouth moved over hers, enticing her to further intimacy, coaxing her to open up to him, pressing her closer so she could feel every inch of his long, lean body.

She opened her mouth, and even though she wasn't a total novice—she had kissed boys a long time ago before her life had been reduced to staying in the shadows—she wasn't prepared for Gabriel's expertise.

His mouth and tongue demanded a response she wasn't sure how to give. She could only react instinctively. Tasting, exploring. Mimicking his movements. She felt rather than heard a growl deep in his throat as he pulled her even closer, delved deeper.

She couldn't breathe, couldn't think, but she knew she never wanted this moment to end. She'd never experienced anything so thrilling. Transporting.

When Gabriel took his mouth off hers she moved with him, loath to let the contact end. Her heart was pounding.

It was a struggle to open her eyes. When she did, it took her a second to focus. Both her hands were clinging to his shirt. She was pressed so close against him that she could feel his desire, long and thick, against her belly.

It should have shocked her. But she pressed closer in an instinctive move, emboldened by a feminine rush of confidence she'd never known before. By the evidence of this man wanting her.

He smiled, but it wasn't a gentle smile. It was hard. Knowing.

Not even that could dent Leonora's desire. She wanted this man to be her first lover, so that whatever happened next she'd always have this experience locked inside her. That was why she'd said *yes*. Because she'd realised how close she'd come to never experiencing this.

'Make love to me, Gabriel.'

He picked up one of her hands and interlocked his fingers with hers. A pulse throbbed between her legs.

His mouth quirked on one side. 'Your wish is my command.'

Even through the haze of arousal and desire making her feel drunk, Leonora doubted that this man was anyone's to command.

He kept their hands linked and led her from the living area, down a hall and to a door. He opened it and Leonora took in a vast bedroom. In contrast to what she'd seen of the apartment so far, this room was almost ascetic. Nothing but bare white walls and a few pieces of modern furniture.

Gabriel let her hand go to switch on a light. It sent out a warm golden glow, softening the hard edges in the room. She wondered about that. About its starkness. And yet it soothed her, coming from a castle stuffed to the gills with oversized furniture and dark décor more suited to the Middle Ages.

Her eyes fell on the bed—the most decadent thing in the room. Massive, and luxuriously dressed with sumptuous dark grey sheets and pillows. Unashamedly masculine. And modern.

'Come here, Leonora.'

She took her gaze off the bed and looked at Gabriel. She sucked in a breath. He filled the space. She pushed down her trepidation and walked the couple of feet over to where he stood. He was taking his cufflinks out of his shirt and placing them on top of a chest of drawers. She stood before him.

'Take off your jewellery.'

She didn't think. She obeyed. Giving herself up to this night and this man with total commitment. She took out her earrings and placed them down next to his cufflinks. Then she removed the matching bracelet. He'd probably already guessed they weren't real, but she didn't care any more.

'Take off my shirt.'

Leonora stepped closer, some of her bravado faltering as she reached for his buttons and started undoing them, revealing his impressive chest. She hoped he wouldn't notice the faint tremor in her hands. When it was open, she pushed it back and looked. Her mouth went dry. He was more like a warrior than a civilised businessman. Hard muscles. Hair curling over his pectorals and descending in a dark line at the centre of a six-pack to disappear under the waistband of his trousers.

He tugged his shirt off completely, letting it drop to the floor. 'Now you. I want to see you.'

No one had ever seen Leonora naked. Not since she was a child. When she was a teenager, fooling around with boys at after-school parties, it had always been an awkward fumbling in the dark, under clothes. Not this stark *'I want to see you'* while standing in the golden glow of a lamp in front of the most intimidating man in the world. A connoisseur of women, by all accounts.

Before Leonora could overthink it she turned around, presenting Gabriel with her back and the zip to her dress. She pulled her hair over one shoulder and steeled herself for the moment she would feel his hands at her zip. But instead of going there first, his hands landed on her shoulders, and then she felt his breath at the back of her neck, before he pressed his mouth there, the moist tip of his tongue flicking out to taste her skin.

Her legs nearly gave way completely.

She was dealing with a consummate seducer—not an over-eager boy.

His hands trailed over her skin as if he had all the time in the world to learn her shape. Goosebumps popped up even though she was warm. *Hot.* Melting...

Then his hands moved to the top of her dress and he started to pull her zip down, all the way, until it stopped just above the curve of her buttocks. His knuckles brushed her skin there and it felt as intimate as if he'd kissed her.

The dress was loosened around her chest but she brought her arms up, stopping it from falling down.

'Turn around.'

Her heart pounding, Leonora turned. After a moment she looked up and saw Gabriel's face. It was...stark. Hungry. She shivered.

He put his hands on her arms and slowly pulled them apart. The dress stayed up for a moment and then, under its own weight, fell down to her waist. She wore a matching strapless bra. Red lace.

Gabriel let her arms go and reached behind her to undo her bra. It fell away to the floor before she could worry about him noticing how frayed and worn it was.

He looked at her for a long moment. Saying nothing.

And then, 'You are more beautiful than anything I've ever imagined.'

Gabriel reached out and reverently cupped her breasts. Leonora had always felt self-conscious about their size, but they fitted Gabriel's palms perfectly. He rubbed his thumbs across her nipples and she had to bite her lip to stop herself from moaning out loud as they stiffened under his touch, almost to the point of pain.

He stopped for a moment, bringing his hands up to cup her face before seeking her mouth again and drawing her deep into a drugging kiss. Her hand clasped his wrist, needing something, anything, to root herself in this dream.

The friction of her bare breasts against his chest was sensory overload. But that was nothing... He stopped kissing her and trailed his mouth across her jaw and down the side of her neck to her shoulder, and then down to her breast. He cupped the plump flesh again and lifted it to his mouth, teasing her stiffened flesh with his tongue and teeth.

She couldn't stop the moan this time. It came out like a guttural plea to stop...never to stop...to keep going. Her hands were on his head, her fingers in his thick hair as he lavished the same torture on her other breast until they were both tingling and wet from his mouth.

When he stopped and lifted his head Leonora could barely keep standing. Gabriel pushed her dress down the rest of the way, over her hips. It fell to the floor with a barely audible swish of silk.

Now she wore only panties and stockings. Her shoes. She kicked them off, dropping a few inches in height. It made Gabriel seem even taller, more impressive.

Then, before she could worry about how to stay standing on her wobbly legs, she was lifted into the air against his chest and carried over to the bed, where he lay her down as reverently as if she was made of spun glass...

CHAPTER THREE

GABRIEL WASN'T SURE how he'd managed not to ravish Leonora before now, but he knew something was holding him back. Her reticence—which he felt sure had to be an act—was having an effect on him.

For a man who had slept with some of the world's most beautiful women, and who'd been sexually active since he was a teenager, he was finding lately that sexual liaisons had become merely satisfactory. More often than not disappointing. But here, now, he hadn't done much more than kiss Leonora and already he was having the most erotic experience he'd had in a long time. If ever.

His instincts about her had been right. She was exquisite. Every line of her body sleek and perfect. Her skin was like silk. Her breasts were perfectly shaped. And her nipples— His mouth watered again, just at the thought of how they'd tasted and stiffened against his tongue.

She was looking at him with huge eyes. As if she'd never seen a man before. Part of him was irritated that she could get to him with such a rudimentary act—was he so jaded that faux innocence turned him on?

Enough playacting.

Gabriel divested himself of the rest of his clothes.

Leonora watched as Gabriel efficiently undressed, revealing a body honed and densely muscled. And hard.

She couldn't stop her eyes widening on his arousal, thick and long.

He came down on the bed, resting over her on both hands. She suddenly felt trepidatious. What if he noticed straight away how inexperienced she was? What if it hurt? What if he was too—?

'You don't have to do this, you know...'

He bent down and surrounded one still sensitised nipple in the hot wet heat of his mouth. Leonora's back arched.

She panted, 'What...? Do what...?'

He lifted his head, a sexy smile playing around his wicked mouth. 'Put on the innocent act. You don't have to play games to entice me, Leonora. I'm enticed.'

Before she could respond to that he was ministering the same exquisite torture to her other breast. *Act? What act?* She couldn't think straight. Not when he was massaging one breast with his fingers and nipping at the other with his teeth before soothing it with his tongue.

His tongue trailed down under her breasts to her belly, dipping into her navel before moving further. Leonora tensed as he came close to the juncture of her legs. He tucked his fingers under her panties and tugged. She lifted her bottom off the bed in silent acquiescence. He pulled them down her legs and off completely. Then one stocking and the other followed them to the floor.

Now she was totally naked—like him. And yet she didn't feel self-conscious. Just...hungry. Aching. Empty inside. As if something was missing.

He was looking at her, his eyes roving over her body, and her self-consciousness returned. She was suddenly acutely aware that she didn't conform to current beauty trends by waxing every inch of her body. But Gabriel wasn't looking remotely repulsed.

He came down beside her, his hand resting on the cluster of dark curls between her legs. 'I like a woman to look like a woman.'

He kissed her then, stopping any words or more coherent thoughts. The feeling of pleasure that he liked her as she was quickly became something far more urgent as he pushed her legs apart and his hand explored further, through those tight curls to the secret place where she ached for his touch.

She gasped into his mouth when his seeking fingers found her, wet and ready. He massaged her, stroking her with expert fingers into a level of excitement that had her arching off the bed, pleading incoherently for something just out of reach, a shimmering promise of ecstasy she could almost taste.

He was relentless, teasing her to the point where she thought she would die if he didn't just—

But then, with one deep thrust and a twist of his fingers, Leonora was finally released from the tension, and she soared high on a wave of pleasure so exquisite she cried out, her hands instinctively reaching for Gabriel's wrist to stop his movements, her throbbing flesh over-sensitised.

Gabriel looked down at Leonora, transfixed by the pleasure suffusing her face. Her skin was dewed with perspiration, her cheeks pink. When she looked at him her eyes were unfocused.

'That was… That was…'

He shook his head, trying to fathom how she could manufacture a response so…earthy. Responsive.

He answered for her. 'That was amazing.'

It had been. And he was literally hanging on to the last shred of his control. Seeing her like this, her breasts moving up and down jerkily with her breaths, long dark hair tumbled across the pillow, it was all he could do to find and roll on protection.

He settled between her legs, where the core of her body was still hot and damp. She looked at him, her mouth swollen from his kisses. He'd never seen a more erotic sight, had never felt such a visceral need to join with a woman.

He couldn't wait any longer.

He put his hands on her hips, positioned himself where she was so wet and ready, and plunged deep into the hottest, tightest embrace he'd ever known.

The sensation was so exquisite that he almost climaxed in that moment.

It was also unexpected.

She was innocent.

Unbelievably.

Her eyes were wide and shocked. He saw her silent entreaty to move...to do something to alleviate this alien sensation. And Gabriel could no more deny her that silent plea than he could force his mind back to some rational place and absorb this revelation fully.

It took supreme skill and control to claw himself back from the brink and move slowly in and out...

Leonora's brain was white-hot with the sudden pain of Gabriel's body thrusting into hers and now, as the pain ebbed, with the building of a whole new level of tension. He'd looked at her just now as if he'd realised she was a virgin, but to her profound relief he hadn't said anything...

She didn't want him to say a word to take them out of this moment. She was joined with this man who had taken her over, body and soul. He lifted her buttocks up, so he could deepen his thrusts, and every single part of her body spasmed with a wave of pleasure, cancelling out any last vestige of pain.

He caught her hands, both of them, and twined his fingers with hers. He brought them over her head and held them there as he moved in and out in a relentless rhythm that made her writhe against him, seeking release from the growing tension.

She could do nothing but hold on as he wound her so high she thought she would break into a million pieces—and then, with no warning, she did break apart, on a thrust so deep that she gasped at the majesty of his body pulsing deep inside hers. She saw an expression of almost pain on his face as he stared down at her, as if he'd never seen a woman before.

Wave upon wave of ecstasy racked her body. She could feel her inner muscles clamping around Gabriel's hard length. She was his captive of pleasure and yet she'd never felt more free as she soared on a high that was breathtaking.

He jerked against her and she bit her lip to stop crying out as yet another mini-orgasm wrenched her apart all over again.

She had been so totally unprepared for this overload of sensation that she didn't even notice when Gabriel extricated himself from her embrace, slipping into the deep oblivion of deep and total satisfaction...

When Leonora woke the faint light of dawn was painting its pink trails across the sky. It took her a second to absorb the fact that she wasn't in her own bed and that she felt different.

Because she was different.

She was no longer a virgin. She had been thoroughly initiated into the art of lovemaking by a master.

She turned her head and saw Gabriel's dark one beside her. Even in sleep he looked powerful. Her gaze moved down his naked body hungrily, lingering over the densely packed muscles of his abdomen and lower, to where his masculinity looked no less impressive at rest.

Her lower body clenched. After they'd made love that first time she'd fallen into a pleasure coma. And then she'd woken a couple of hours later with her bottom tucked into Gabriel's body, his growing erection stirring against her. He'd demonstrated that that wasn't the only way to bring about intense pleasure and had brought her slowly and inexorably back to life with his hands and his mouth, showing her that what had happened hadn't been a dream.

No. It hadn't been a dream.

It had been very much an explosive and transformative reality. She held the sheet to her body, going cold inside as the full significance of the night sank in. Just hours ago she'd been about to be publicly betrothed to Lazaro Sanchez. And yet here she was, having been thoroughly bedded by a totally different man.

This behaviour was so out of character for her. She hadn't even kissed Lazaro beyond one chaste kiss on the lips. And yet she'd spent mere hours in Gabriel's company and tumbled into bed with him with barely a moment's hesitation.

She'd felt responsible for so long—since her parents had lost everything when she was a teenager—that she'd almost forgotten what it was like to want something just for herself. And now she felt supremely selfish. The paparazzi had probably been camped outside the *castillo* all night, while she'd been here indulging in sheer sensual decadence.

She felt as if millennia had passed since the previous day, when she'd set out from her home ready to commit to Lazaro Sanchez. And here she was in another man's bed.

She put a hand to her burning face.

She thought of how Gabriel had looked at her with that single-minded intensity. No one had ever looked at her like that before. As if they truly *saw* her. As a woman. Independent of her name and the scandal that had rocked her family.

And then she cursed herself.

Gabriel Torres was an experienced man of the world. A consummate lover. He probably looked at all his lovers like that. She was just one in a long line. She'd intrigued him last night, but even if he hadn't figured out she'd been a virgin she doubted very much he'd be expecting to see her again.

Terrified that he would wake and look at her, and see how profoundly he'd affected her, she stole out of the bed as quietly as she could. She held her breath when he moved, saying something incomprehensible in his sleep. When he didn't wake Leonora gathered up her things and tiptoed out of the bedroom, finding a guest suite down the hall where she dressed and repaired herself as best she could.

She avoided looking at herself in the mirror. She tried to ignore the tenderness between her legs. But then she caught a glimpse of the redness around her jaw and neck. The burn from Gabriel's stubble. The burn of shame.

She quickly pulled her hair back and tied it into a rough bun. She put her wrap around herself, hiding as much of the evidence of the passion of the night as possible. Then she crept out of the apartment and down to the lobby, where she got the concierge to call her a taxi.

Thankfully she didn't have to wait long. As it drove through the quiet early-morning streets she took a deep, shuddering breath, hating the awful bereft feeling stealing over her.

She thought of the man sprawled sexily in bed in his stunning apartment. He would wake up and get on with his life and not think about her again. Of that she was sure. Last night would barely register on his radar. How could it when she'd been such a novice?

She'd made a pact with the devil, agreeing to sleep with

Gabriel Torres, telling herself that one night would be enough. Because now the empty feeling inside her mocked her. One night with Gabriel Torres had ruined her for ever.

Gabriel woke slowly, through layers of a deep sense of satisfaction. Not just any satisfaction. Sexual satisfaction. It was a long time since he'd felt like this.

His mouth curved into a smile as images came tumbling back into his head. Long dark hair, elegant curves, high, firm breasts with deliciously hard nipples... Brown curls covering the apex between her legs—the place where he'd lost himself and found ecstasy. The best sex he'd ever had.

With a virgin.

His eyes snapped open on that thought and he jack-knifed up in the bed, instantly awake.

She'd been a virgin.

He hadn't been able to process that information fully in the midst of the hottest experience of his life. She hadn't asked him to stop. She'd entreated him to go on with those huge grey eyes. And he'd tipped over the edge of his legendary control.

Uncomfortably, he had to concede now that he didn't think it had been her innocence that had elevated the experience beyond the realms of normality. It had been *her*. And their unique chemistry. He'd had no idea it would be so explosive.

Where was she?

There was a stillness in the bedroom that extended out into the apartment. He stood up from the bed and pulled on a pair of jeans, and only then noticed that it was bright outside. Already morning. He could hear the faint hum of city traffic.

He felt discombobulated. He always woke at dawn, if not before. He never slept in.

He padded through the apartment, an uneasy and unfamiliar feeling of exposure sliding into his gut.

There was no sign of her. Literally no sign. Had he dreamt it all? Then he saw the small tumbler that still held some alcohol. He didn't like the sense of relief.

He went back into his bedroom and something glinted in the morning light on his cabinet. Her jewellery. She'd left it behind. He went over and picked it up and recognised instantly that it wasn't real. Costume jewellery. To create a façade.

Leonora Flores de la Vega. The heiress with nothing to her name except her name. And her astonishing beauty. A virgin who'd left him behind in his bed.

No woman ever left him. *He* left women. And no woman left him with this hungry, clawing ache of need.

Even after only one night he could sense that the more he had of her, the more he would want. Unprecedented. One night with her was not enough. Not nearly enough.

As he stood under the powerful spray of his shower a few minutes later Gabriel knew that Leonora Flores was not like his usual women. There was a wildness under her serene exterior and it resonated with something inside him—a wild streak he never allowed to surface in his day-to-day life, when he had to be supremely controlled and on guard at all times. Too many people depended on him.

He'd been her first lover. And he couldn't deny that, along with the erotic charge he felt thinking of that, he also felt something else totally uncharacteristic. *Possessive.* It had been there the previous evening too, when he'd felt the electric current between them as she'd stood beside Sanchez with his arm around her waist.

Gabriel emerged from the shower and slung a towel around his waist. He caught a glimpse of himself in the mirror over the sink and stopped, looking long and hard at his reflection. He was thirty-three years old. He'd been ignoring his advisors' not so subtle whispers for some time now. Whispers that had been getting more insistent. Whispers about settling down. Putting forward a more respectable image. Being a family man.

Something lodged in Gabriel's gut at that thought. *Family man.* He'd always known that he would have to have a family some day. After all, he was the last in his line. But after his emotionally sterile upbringing, with two parents who had despised each other, he'd never relished the prospect.

And he'd never fully admitted to himself that while the thought of a family terrified him on one level, on another he'd always wondered if he could do it any differently? He'd grown up with one assertion—never to bring children into this world and leave them to their fate as his own parents had.

His younger sister had suffered more than he had, and he still felt guilty that he hadn't noticed her descent into chaos. But by then he'd been the only thing holding the Cruz y Torres empire together...

Both his parents had conducted extramarital affairs for as long as he could remember, and he'd routinely witnessed them lying to each other about their activities to the point when it had become farcical.

Gabriel was ashamed to recall that when he had been much younger, he'd had a fantasy of a relationship far removed from what he'd seen with his parents. Uncynical. Respectful. Kind. But life had shown him that he was a fool to have such dreams when he'd found his first lover in bed with his so-called best friend.

She'd told Gabriel she'd seduced his friend to make Gabriel jealous. He'd thrown his lover and his best friend out, and from that day forward had ruthlessly quashed his silly teenage fantasies.

But perhaps he had finally met someone with whom he could envisage embarking on the next phase of his life. He wasn't such a fool as to equate physical innocence with honesty, but there was something special and unique about Leonora Flores de la Vega.

She was stunningly beautiful, and she oozed elegance and class in spite of the fact that she was all but penniless. They had the most insane chemistry Gabriel had ever experienced with a woman.

And clearly, if she'd been prepared to marry Lazaro Sanchez, she was in the market for marriage.

The thought of her with that man made Gabriel's hands clench into fists. His expression in the mirror turned hard.

Sanchez had obviously been ready to make a lifelong commitment in a bid to garner respect. Perhaps it was a sign that Gabriel finally needed to deal with something he'd been pushing away for a long time. Saying a curt *Not yet* whenever another advisor tentatively mentioned the notion of settling down.

But maybe 'not yet' had become now.

Leonora Flores de la Vega was perfect on every level for what he envisaged in a marriage. He had never been so old-fashioned as to have expected a virginal wife, but he couldn't deny that her innocence appealed to a deeply masculine part of him. As did the knowledge that she hadn't slept with Sanchez.

She was from *their* world. She knew how these marriages worked. And after last night he didn't have to worry about compatibility.

Last night he hadn't seduced Leonora for any other reason than because he wanted her. Sanchez had been the last person on his mind. But now...

He relished the perfection of timing and serendipity. And the opportunity to show Lazaro Sanchez in a very comprehensive way that a woman like Leonora Flores de la Vega was out of his league.

For ever.

When Leonora arrived back at the *castillo* after driving Matías back to his school, she found her mother waiting for her, looking pale and agitated.

'What is it? Is it Papá?'

Leonora always had the fear that something would set her father off again. Something like this—his daughter getting jilted in public by her fiancé.

Her mother shook her head. 'No, nothing like that. Papá is having a nap. You got a phone call...from Gabriel Torres. He wants you to call him back.'

Her mother was handing her a note with a number on it before Leonora could fully register it. It had been two days since that cataclysmic night. Two days of feeling alternately shocked and shamed and giddy at what had happened. And two days of the knowledge sinking in that of *course* Gabriel wasn't going to be chasing her down.

Except now butterflies exploded in her belly. Along with a far more carnal tug of awareness. And the man wasn't even here.

She looked at the number. A cell phone number.

Her mother gripped her arm. 'Oh, Leo—*Gabriel Torres*. You must have made an impression.'

Leonora's face burned and she avoided her mother's eye. She'd been vague about Gabriel's involvement the other night, making it sound as if he'd just offered her a place to hide out. But she knew he'd offered her so much more. And delivered.

She scrabbled for something to say. 'Mamá, I'm sure

he's getting in touch for something quite boring. Let me go and call him back.'

Her mother shooed her off, two bright pink spots in her cheeks, making her look girlish for her fifty-four years.

Leonora's insides cramped as she went into the castle's office, the administrative centre where they took bookings for tours. Tours that were falling increasingly in numbers because people inevitably wanted to experience something more exciting than just walking around a dusty medieval castle full of antiques and scary-looking portraits of long-dead ancestors and a tired and wilted walled garden.

Her family's dependence on her sat heavily on her shoulders today. She'd just had a painful conversation at Matías's school about overdue fees.

She sat down at the desk and put the piece of paper in front of her. She pulled her cell phone out of her pocket and keyed in his number. For an age she sat there, a little paralysed at the thought of hearing that deep rumble of a voice again.

Then, before she could lose her nerve, she pressed the key and after a second heard the long ring tone.

The call was picked up almost immediately with an impatient, brusque tone. *'Sí?'*

She almost cut off the connection, he sounded so forbidding, and then his tone changed and he said sharply, 'Leonora, is that you?'

She gulped. 'Yes, it's me.'

'Thank you for calling me back.'

She thought she detected a dry tone in his voice. She didn't imagine he had many women doing a disappearing act on him.

'I'm sorry for…for leaving the way I did the other morning…but I felt it was for the best.'

'For who? You? Or me…?'

Leonora squirmed in the chair. 'Both of us… It was—'

She stopped. She'd been about to say *just a moment out of time*, but that sounded far too whimsical.

'It was just one night.'

'An incredible night.'

His voice was low and it seemed to rumble down the phone and across Leonora's skin. Her mouth went dry and her palms got clammy just thinking about it.

Then he said, 'I'd like to take you out for dinner.'

Leonora pushed aside the X-rated memories. 'Dinner?'

'Yes…' He sounded amused.

'When?'

'Tonight. I'll pick you up at seven.'

'I…'

'Do you have plans, Leonora?'

Was it her imagination or was there a mocking tone in his voice now? Of course she didn't have plans—other than the endless worrying about what was to become of them.

She tried to sound as nonchalant as possible. 'No, I don't have plans this evening.'

He became brisk again. 'Good. I'll see you at seven.'

CHAPTER FOUR

By ALMOST SEVEN that evening Leonora was a bag of nerves at the thought of seeing Gabriel again after sharing such intimacies, and also wondering what he wanted. A repeat of that night? Or was he just intrigued because she wasn't like his usual lovers?

The thought had slid into her mind over the past couple of days...wondering if he'd noticed her innocence. But he hadn't said anything. And certainly any pain had been fleeting.

She tensed when she heard the low purr of a powerful engine and crunching gravel, not remotely ready to see the man again.

Liar.

She went to the window and peeked out, feeling like a coward. She watched him step out of a low-slung sports car—a different one from the other night. This was black.

He was dressed semi-casually, in dark trousers and a lighter toned long-sleeved top. She could imagine the material was expensive, the way it moulded to the muscles of his chest as he came around the car.

He looked stern. Austere. But then she remembered how he'd smiled wickedly. Sexily. Her insides spasmed.

She was about to go into the hall to answer the door when he rang the bell, but just then she heard quick footsteps cross the marbled hall and cursed silently. Her mother.

Seizing on the opportunity to meet the man who had been
Leonora's knight in shining armour the other night.

Her mother's disapproval of Lazaro Sanchez's behaviour,
as compared to the gallant actions of one of their own, had
spoken volumes about what she'd really thought of Leonora's first fiancé. And yet, Leonora thought cynically, her
mother would have been only too happy to have Lazaro's
money paying off their debts and restoring their reputation.

The front door opened and Leonora heard voices—her
mother's too high and girlish, and Gabriel's much lower. A
light sweat broke out on her brow. She wished there was a
mirror to check her reflection again.

Her black silk shirt dress with its wide belt had at one
time been fashionable, with its thigh-high slit, but now she
was afraid it was far too provocative and out of date. She
touched the buttons again, to make sure they were done
up as far as they could go—which didn't feel high enough.
And should she have put her hair up?

Footsteps approached and she realised she was clasping
her hands like a schoolteacher. She unclasped them just before the door opened.

Leonora only saw Gabriel, filling the doorway as if this
massive house had been built around him.

Her mother said redundantly, 'Leo, Mr Torres is here.'

Leonora moved forward, shaky in high heels. For a ridiculous moment she wasn't sure if she should put out her
hand to shake his, but then he reached for her, taking her
shoulders in his hands and bending down to kiss her on
each cheek.

His scent caught her unawares, hurtling her back in time
to the other evening. She put her hands up to his arms—in
a bid to stay standing as much as anything else.

'Señorita de la Vega. Thank you for agreeing to come
and have dinner with me.'

There was a tone in his voice that made her look at him. Intimate. Complicit. It sent a flash of heat between her legs.

He straightened up and let her go. 'Shall we?'

Leonora gave her mother a quick kiss and walked out ahead of Gabriel while he exchanged a few parting words with her mother. He came out and opened the passenger door of the car, waiting until she got in. She tried to gather herself as he came around the car and got in.

He sat behind the wheel. But instead of starting the car he looked at her and said, *'Leo?'*

It took her a second to understand his meaning. 'Matías called me Leo when he was small. It kind of stuck...in spite of my father's distaste for shortening names.'

Leonora couldn't look away from those mesmerising gold-flecked eyes. His jaw was clean-shaven, but she could still remember the way her skin had felt so tender after kissing him. It had burned. Like she burned now...deep inside.

'Leo...' he said. Slowly. Testing it out. And then, 'I like it. It suits you. Makes me think of a lioness.'

His mouth curved into a small smile and then he turned the ignition on and drove down the drive and out of the property.

Leonora was breathless. So much for trying to regain her composure. She'd never thought driving a car could be considered sexy, but watching the way Gabriel drove, with nonchalant confidence, was undeniably compelling.

She was able to study him as he drove, taking in the thick hair swept back off his forehead. The long aquiline nose, more than hinting at his exclusive lineage. The hard jaw and that sensual mouth, made for sin. And that powerful body. Hard and honed. Not an ounce of spare muscle.

A warrior's body in the guise of a very modern man. All in all, an intoxicating package.

He glanced at her and she looked away, face burning.

She realised her thigh was bared in the slit of the dress and hurriedly pulled it together, holding it with her hand.

'I've seen your thigh, Leonora.'

Her face burned hotter. She didn't know how to handle this…this flirting.

She blurted out, 'The other night… It wasn't… I don't usually behave like that.'

Something shifted in the atmosphere as Gabriel pulled up smoothly to a red traffic light. She risked a look at him and saw he was staring straight ahead, hands on the wheel.

'I thought as much,' he said after a moment, the car moving forward again.

Now she felt even more exposed. Clearly her inexperience had been woefully obvious. But hopefully not the full extent of it.

'Why didn't you tell me you were a virgin?'

Leonora felt the blood drain from her face. From hot to cold in seconds. 'How did you know?' she asked through bloodless lips.

Thankfully Gabriel needed to focus on the traffic, so he was looking ahead and not at her.

'Because I've never slept with a virgin before.'

Leonora wanted to slip down in the seat and disappear altogether, drowning in a pool of humiliation. But she forced herself to sit straight.

'Why did you ask me out this evening if you know I'm such a novice? I'm sure there are many women who can provide more experienced entertainment.'

She felt him glance at her but she stared straight ahead.

'You misunderstand me, Leonora. I did not say this was a negative thing.' He waited a moment and then he said, in a low voice that rubbed along every nerve-ending, 'In fact it was the most erotic experience of my life.'

That made Leonora even more rigid. 'If you've asked

me out because I'm some kind of novelty to you—' Her
flow of words halted when Gabriel swung abruptly into a
layby and he came to a stop.

She looked at him and he turned to face her, the car
idling. He looked stern and she swallowed.

'I did not ask you out because you're a novelty. I asked
you out because I desire you very much.'

His gaze dropped to her mouth and he muttered something unintelligible to himself. Then, before she knew
what was happening, he closed the distance between them,
snaked a hand under her hair to the back of her neck and
his mouth was on hers, possessing her so thoroughly that
by the time he broke the kiss she was pressed against him,
hands clutching at his jacket.

She was gasping, dizzy. After mere seconds. Her mouth
throbbed. His kiss had been swift and explicitly sexual.

He raised a brow. 'That is no novelty. That is the kind
of chemistry and desire that comes along very rarely. Trust
me. And I want much more than one night with you, Leonora—much more.'

Leonora couldn't speak as Gabriel pulled back out into
the traffic as if nothing had happened, his enigmatic com-
ment reverberating in her head.

I want much more than one night...

What was he proposing? An affair? For her to become
his mistress?

Everything in her balked at that because she knew she
was not mistress material. She was a world away from
the sophisticated women of the world he would know, in
spite of her privileged upbringing. Until they'd lost all that
privilege.

But then maybe he was only talking in terms of days...
weeks. Gabriel Torres didn't flaunt his affairs. He was dis-
cretion personified—which was largely how he'd built up

such a mythical reputation. And a man like him wouldn't be satisfied with one woman for long.

It was only when she saw that they were veering away from the city centre that she asked, 'Where are we going?'

He glanced at her and she felt it like a searing brand. *Dios.*

'We're going to my home. My family home.'

'Castillo Torres?'

Leonora was immediately intimidated. She'd visited the estate a few times in her lifetime, for social events with her parents. That long-ago polo match. Fundraisers. Galas. She hadn't been in a long time, but she remembered it as being a huge and intimidatingly grand place.

In comparison, it made her own family *castillo* look like a cosy country cottage.

'Yes. I trust that is okay?'

Leonora nodded. 'Of course.'

The truth was that even if he'd taken her to a busy restaurant full of people it wouldn't have lessened his intensity, or his power to intimidate. Maybe this was how he flew under the radar? He kept his liaisons confined to his elegant apartment or the *castillo*. Well out of the public eye.

Leonora didn't like to think that she was the latest in a long line of women who had been invited back to the *castillo*, but she told herself she was being ridiculous. There was a long line of women before her and there would undoubtedly be a long line after her. She didn't see a man like Gabriel Torres settling down to a life of domesticity any time soon.

She couldn't even imagine him in such a milieu.

He was turning off the main road now, onto a smaller road which led to a huge set of iron gates that opened automatically as soon as they drove up to them. Gabriel lowered his window and saluted the security guard in the box on the other side of the gate.

Leonora's family used to have security at their *castillo*— not any more. There was nothing of value left.

They drove in and Leonora tried not to let her jaw drop at the verdant splendour of the grounds. Tall trees lined the drive and beyond she could see lush landscaped lawns and blooming bougainvillea.

The winding drive opened into a massive courtyard with a fountain in the middle, behind which the *castillo* rose majestically. Not unlike Leonora's home, but on a far grander scale, it had a distinctly Moorish shape. And she noticed immediately that it was in pristine condition, which made her heart ache as she acknowledged how far her family had fallen.

Gabriel stopped the car at the bottom of the steps leading up to the main door. He got out and came around the bonnet, opening Leonora's door and helping her out.

A young man materialised seemingly out of nowhere and Gabriel tossed him the keys, asking him at the same time how his exams had gone.

The young man grinned and said, 'Passed them all, boss!'

Gabriel responded, 'Good for you,' and the young man jumped into the car and drove it around to the back of the *castillo*—presumably to a garage similar to the one under Gabriel's apartment, filled with expensive sports cars.

Keeping her hand in his, Gabriel led her up the steps. The door opened as they approached, as if by magic, and a uniformed butler bowed to them as she stepped over the threshold.

Gabriel said, 'Ernesto I'd like you to meet Leonora Flores de la Vega. Leonora, this is Ernesto, the only person holding this whole place together.'

'Not true, sir, but thank you. Señorita de la Vega, pleased to meet you.'

He bowed again and Leonora was charmed. She smiled shyly, 'Lovely to meet you too.'

She liked the way Gabriel acknowledged his staff. She was ashamed to remember how her parents had treated their own as very much beneath them. And now they had none. Karma?

Her hand was still in Gabriel's as he led her through a vast stone hall and out to an inner courtyard with a pool filled with colourful fish and lotus flowers. Stone pillars around the edges led up to a balcony running around the space.

Then they walked through to the other side and back into the main building, where another reception area led off to more rooms and a grand staircase up to the first level.

'This is...beautiful. I was here before, but only in the grounds.'

Gabriel stopped walking and grimaced as he looked around them. 'I've been working on bringing it into the modern era. For years it was dark and dank, full of useless antiques and mouldering paintings of long-dead relatives.'

Leonora couldn't help a small wry smile. 'That sounds like *my* family home.'

She caught Gabriel's eye and his gaze dropped to her mouth. Suddenly he looked...*hungry*. Leonora's heart thumped. Was he going to kiss her right here? Now? She wasn't ready—

But then the look on his face passed and he kept walking, saying, 'It's a painstaking and expensive process. I've been working on this for the last decade and we're not nearly finished.'

Leonora stayed silent, following where he led her, through a confusing labyrinth of corridors. She could see now why he might like his very sparse and elegant city apartment. It was a direct contrast to what he'd grown up with. That was why *she'd* liked it.

A sense of affinity struck her again...disconcerting.

They were approaching the end of the corridor now, and Gabriel pushed open a door which led into a massive drawing room, full of light and huge windows that looked out over the back of the *castillo*. All she could see was acres of lush green, trees, and what looked like an orchard in the distance.

'We grow lemons and olives here. Sell them to an organic company. Part of my restoration is an attempt to make the *castillo* and its grounds as self-sufficient and environmentally friendly as possible.'

He let her hand go and went over to a drinks cabinet.

Leonora said wistfully, 'That's what I'd love to do too. The day when these kinds of buildings can justify themselves by merely existing has surely ended.'

He cast her a look over his shoulder. 'Exactly.'

He came back then, with a glass of what looked like champagne in one hand and water in the other.

He handed her the tall elegant flute and said, 'Dinner will be ready in a short while, but first I have a proposal to put to you.'

Leonora took a sip of champagne and it fizzed down her throat. She swallowed, genuinely intrigued. 'A proposal?'

He looked at her carefully. 'Yes, Leonora. A proposal. Of marriage.'

CHAPTER FIVE

A PROPOSAL OF MARRIAGE. If Leonora had still had some of the champagne in her mouth or her throat she would have choked or spat it out. The shock of his words thumped her in the gut. She felt winded.

He was just looking at her. Assessing. As if he *hadn't* just said the most audacious thing she'd ever heard. A sliver of ice went down her back when she thought of the possibility that she might have hallucinated briefly.

'Did you just say—?'

He cut in smoothly. 'That I'm proposing marriage? Yes, I did.'

Leonora clutched the glass as if it was a lifeline. Her brain wouldn't seem to work. It felt sluggish.

'Do you…? *Why?*'

'For many reasons—chief of which is because I think we'd be a good match. I've known for some time now that I need to settle down, but it's always been an unpalatable prospect…until we met and connected.'

Connected.

Leonora's head was suddenly filled with X-rated images of them in bed, limbs entangled, his powerful body thrusting in and out of hers, transporting her to heights of ecstasy she'd dreamed about every night since.

Something else struck her and she felt slightly sick. 'Is

this just because I was a…a virgin? Maybe you're old-fash-ioned and that kind of thing—'

He held a hand up, eyes sparking. 'Stop right there. This has nothing to do with your sexual innocence.' He low-ered his hand. 'Although I have to admit that knowing I was your first lover is incredibly satisfying in a way that I never would have thought possible.'

Leonora's insides clenched. She had to admit that losing her innocence under the expert tutelage of Gabriel hadn't exactly been *un*satisfying. Far from it. But…*marriage*? And yet why should it be such an alien concept when she'd agreed to marry someone else only recently?

She struggled to understand Gabriel's motivation. 'But I'm not remotely suitable.'

He frowned. 'You couldn't be *more* suitable for my re-quirements.'

Requirements.

A cold weight lodged in her chest. And it mocked her. Because she realised that for a moment she'd fantasised that this might be a proposal stemming from emotion. Feel-ings. When she'd never even considered that with Lazaro Sanchez.

But you didn't sleep with him, reminded a small voice.

Leonora lifted her chin. 'Do I need to remind you that my family are considered pariahs in society? We haven't been invited to an event in years. I don't see you sullying the Cruz y Torres name by association with us.'

In answer he pulled out his phone from his trouser pocket and after a few seconds handed it to her, 'Have you seen this?'

'This' was a grainy paparazzi picture of her getting into his car that night outside the hotel. She looked like a rabbit caught in the headlights and he was staring directly down the lens of the camera, defiantly.

She handed it back, feeling sick. 'I tend to avoid looking at those websites or their headlines, considering my family were their sole fodder at one time.'

'I'm showing it to you to illustrate my point that I really don't care what anyone thinks of us getting together.'

Leonora looked at him. 'What would your parents think?'

Gabriel's expression hardened. 'My parents are not remotely involved in the running of my life and haven't been since before I came of age. If anything, I run *their* lives. My father spends most of his time in his city townhouse and at this point in time I'm not even sure where my mother is—she usually has the decency to conduct her illicit liaisons in discreet locations. They have no jurisdiction over me.'

Leonora shivered slightly, recalling how serious he'd been at twenty-one. No wonder, if he'd been running a massive business on his own.

'Don't you have a sister? Younger than you?'

His expression immediately softened. The cold weight in Leonora's chest warmed slightly.

'Yes. Estella. The bane of my existence.'

And yet clearly she wasn't, if that softened look was anything to go by.

Intrigued, Leonora asked, 'Where is she?'

'She's in New York, working as a model. She went through a rough patch a few years ago. Fell in with the wrong people. But she's doing really well now.'

The pride in his voice was evident. Then his focus came back to Leonora.

He said, 'Your family might have fallen from grace due to your father's actions, but whose grace? And who else hasn't? I despise that hypocrisy.'

At that moment there was a discreet knock on the door

and Leonora looked around to see Ernesto enter. 'Dinner is ready, Señor Torres.'

'Thank you, we'll be right there.'

Leonora turned back to Gabriel, still feeling slightly winded, absorbing his words. She would never have expected him not to care about his family's reputation, but conceded cynically that he had that luxury because they were so powerful.

He said, 'I know you weren't expecting this when I brought you here, but I don't believe in playing games, Leonora. Life is too short. You're the first woman I've ever brought to the *castillo*. And you're the first woman I've ever proposed to.'

Gabriel was not used to being unable to read a woman easily. Usually they were so *unsubtle*. But Leonora was like the Sphinx. All cool and serene. He'd put a marriage proposal to her and she'd recovered quickly after her initial shock.

Their dinner plates had just been cleared away by his housekeeper and he asked, 'Did you go to university?'

A faint wash of colour came into her cheeks. She avoided looking at him and he had to curb the urge to tip her chin up so she had no choice. Once again, not usually an issue for him with women.

She shook her head. 'No. I wanted to do a business degree, but by the time I left school...things had changed. Matías was in school, but he came home every weekend and he needed me. And I had to work at the *castillo*—try to get it to make us some money.'

'I can imagine that experience probably taught you as much as a business degree.'

Leonora smiled ruefully. 'Perhaps, although it hasn't exactly been a resounding success. The *castillo* needs serious investment—like what you're doing here.'

Gabriel seized the opportunity she'd presented him with. 'I can help you with that kind of investment, Leonora.'

Now she looked at him, eyes wide, the flush in her face deepening. She stuttered, 'That isn't... I didn't mean to make it sound like—'

'I know you didn't. I'm merely stating a fact. If you become my wife, naturally your security and your family's, and the restoration of your *castillo*, become my responsibility.'

His cool, emotionless logic and the word *responsibility* made something snap inside Leonora. She blurted out, 'Why do you want to marry now?'

He sat back and looked at her. 'To be perfectly honest, because you're the first woman I've met who has inspired me to consider it.'

Leonora felt light-headed. 'Me? I inspired you?'

She really wasn't that special.

'I always knew I'd have to marry. I'm the last in my line. Not marrying and not having a family isn't an option for me. But it's something I've preferred not to think about. Until now.'

'But if it was an option you'd prefer not to?'

'I don't deal in *what ifs* or unknowns. I deal with reality, and this is my reality. And yours too, Leonora. Or are you going to tell me your engagement to Sanchez was born out of emotion or desire?'

Leonora flushed. 'No, of course not.'

She felt exposed, and tense. He knew full well she hadn't slept with Lazaro.

A sense of something that felt like hurt compelled her to push back. 'What makes you think I'm available? Just because I agreed to marry Lazaro? The other night you were reminding me that we're bound by duty and responsibility, but maybe I want more than that. Maybe I don't want to just become someone's *responsibility*.'

Or, maybe, she realised in the same split second, she didn't want to become Gabriel Torres's responsibility, because already she was feeling things for him that were dangerous and disturbing.

Gabriel sat forward. 'Are you telling me that you hadn't agreed to let Lazaro Sanchez take responsibility for your family's debts?'

At that moment the housekeeper came back into the room with a tray that held coffee for Gabriel and tea for Leonora.

Without taking his gaze from Leonora's, Gabriel said, 'We'll take it in the lounge, thank you, Tulia.'

He stood up and Leonora followed his lead from the dining room, glad of a momentary reprieve from the growing tension.

They followed the housekeeper into another surprisingly airy room, adjacent to the dining room. Sunset was bathing everything in a pink and golden hue. The furniture was classic, elegant. Timeless.

The woman set the tray down on a coffee table between two couches.

Gabriel said, 'Thank you, Tulia. That will be all.'

The woman left the room.

Gabriel said, 'Please, sit down.'

Leonora hesitated for a moment, torn between telling Gabriel that she wanted to leave, so she could get out of his disturbing orbit, and the stronger pull to stay. Hear him out.

Let him seduce you again?

Leonora sat down quickly before he might see the turmoil he'd unleashed inside her. Before he could see the want. Even now, despite his disturbing proposition. *Proposal.*

Thankfully he sat down on the opposite couch. She felt as if she could get her breath back and gather her wits as long as he kept his distance. She picked up her cup of tea and took a sip, hoping it would ground her.

He seemed to be waiting for her to speak. It unnerved her. She hadn't had so much focused attention on her from anyone, ever. And from a man like Gabriel Torres it was more than a little overwhelming.

She looked at him. He was sitting back, holding his tiny espresso cup in one big hand but looking no less masculine. One arm was stretched out along the couch, pulling his top tight across his tautly muscled chest.

She swallowed. *Focus.*

'Why do you want to marry me when you could marry any number of far more suitable women?'

He took his arm down and sat forward. A muscle ticked in his jaw. 'Why are you resisting my proposal when you agreed to marry a man you hadn't even slept with?'

Leonora tensed even more—so much that she felt as if she might splinter into a million tiny pieces. It was precisely because she'd slept with Gabriel that she was resisting this proposal. Because she was still reeling after what had happened and how explosive it had been.

She put her cup down and stood up, pride stiffening her spine. 'Maybe I should go. Just because I agreed to marry one man, it does not mean that I'm automatically going to agree to marry the next man who asks me.'

She turned, but stopped when she felt Gabriel's hand on her arm. Gentle, but with enough force to stop her. Reluctantly she faced him, and he let her arm go. She was surprised to see an expression of humility on his face.

'Wait—please.'

He ran a hand through his hair, mussing it up. It gave

him a more approachable air. Less stern. Despite herself, Leonora felt something inside her weaken.

He said, 'I haven't articulated myself very well. Just hear me out…please?'

Leonora had the sense that this didn't happen very often with a man like Gabriel. She nodded her head slightly and sat down.

He sat down again too, but sat forward, with his hands clasped between his legs. He looked at her.

'It was not my intention to make you feel as though I thought of you as a wife for hire, based on your recent history. As I told you, there's been pressure on me for some time to marry and start a family, but no woman has ever made me feel remotely inclined to do so—until the other night and *you*. Every moment in your company only makes me feel more sure that this is the right decision for both of us.'

Leonora cursed him silently. His deep mesmeric voice was drawing her in, making it all sound so reasonable. Logical.

'You know this world, Leo, and you know how to navigate it. I think you share my disdain for it, and yet understand that we need it too. We are bound to it whether we like it or not.'

Leo. She should feel irritated by the way he'd shortened her name—only ever done by her family—but, dammit, she *liked* it. It felt intimate in a way that it didn't feel with her family. Private.

'You and your family need urgent financial help. Matías can't afford to stay at that school for ever. And what will you do if the bank takes your *castillo* as payment for the debts still outstanding?'

Leonora went cold inside. 'How do you know about Matías's school?'

'I know someone with a child in that school, so I know how expensive it is.'

Leonora refused to let herself feel vulnerable. 'I'm sure if we lost everything and Matías had to come out of the school we'd manage.'

'I don't doubt *you* would. But would they? Your parents? Who have only known a life of privilege and luxury, even in spite of what's happened? And would Matías survive without the care of special teachers and assistants? You'd have to work—you wouldn't be there all the time.'

Leonora knew he was right. Her parents would never survive in the real world, in a small apartment—if they were lucky enough even to get one. Neither would Matías. She had less sympathy for her parents, but Matías... She'd do anything for him. To keep him safe and secure.

Gabriel said, 'And there's something else you're not ac-knowledging.'

His voice was lower. Seductive. Leonora really wanted to avoid his dark, knowing gaze, but she couldn't.

She feigned nonchalance even as her skin tingled with anticipation. 'What's that?'

She knew, though.

She knew with every gathering rush of heat that pulsed through her body.

'We want each other.'

Just that. Stark. To the point.

'I don't like to play games, Leonora, life is too short.'

'And believe me,' he said, 'that's as solid a reason as any to embark on marriage. We have social compatibility and mutual chemistry. A powerful combination.'

Not really understanding why she felt such a need to re-sist his pull, Leonora said, 'But it won't last—it never does, does it? And what then?'

Gabriel raised a brow. 'This wasn't a concern of yours

when you agreed to marry Sanchez? A man you hadn't even slept with?'

Leonora stood up abruptly, feeling cornered. She paced away to a window that took in the expanse of the *castillo*'s impressive back lawn. She was being a total hypocrite—she knew she was. And she was deluding herself. She *did* know why she was resisting his pull. But how could she explain that she had found it easier to agree to marry a man she hadn't been intimate with, who she hadn't even wanted, than *this* man, with whom she had been intimate and who she did want, with a hunger that made her feel so many things it was overwhelming?

She realised that Gabriel was infinitely more disturbing to her on so many levels because he affected not only her equilibrium, physically, but also her emotions. She'd grown up in a world where you kept your emotions hidden behind a polite front.

Her parents had never really approved of Leonora and Matías's affectionate relationship. But Matías didn't understand about keeping his emotions hidden and Leonora loved him for that. When her parents had sent Matías to the special school they'd told her that it was because he was becoming too attached to her. Too dependent. She'd always felt guilty that her need for his uncomplicated love and affection was the reason he'd been sent away, and while she knew now that he'd been sent away for lots of other reasons, to do with his own self-development in the right environment, she still felt guilty about that need in her for emotional sustenance. As if it was a weakness.

And that was why Gabriel scared her. Because he touched on those needs and wants inside her. That was why it had been easy to say yes to Lazaro. Because he hadn't disturbed her emotions on any level...

* * *

Gabriel looked at Leonora's graceful, willowy form. She oozed elegance in spite of the tense lines of her body. She was perfect. For him. For his life. And yet she resisted.

Irritation spiked in his gut when he thought of how she'd been willing to marry Sanchez with far less to go on.

He stood up and walked over to stand beside her. Her arms were crossed tightly over her chest. The irritation got stronger.

Before he could stop himself he said, 'Were you in love with Sanchez? Is that what this is about?'

She turned to look at him and he saw shock on her face. 'No! How can you even ask that? You really think I would have slept with you if I'd loved him?'

Gabriel didn't like the way her words soothed something jagged inside him. *Jealousy.*

She bit her lip. 'I just… I'm ashamed to admit it now, but I think I found it easier to make a commitment to him because it felt like a sterile business agreement. It's not as if I'm under any illusions. I know that people like us have to marry for reasons that are far removed from love…but I hadn't expected that I would…*want* my husband.'

Gabriel clenched his hand into a fist by his side to avoid reaching out to touch her. She reminded him of a nervy foal. Ready to bolt at the slightest sound.

'Is that such a bad thing?'

She looked at him and her eyes were dark pools of grey, searching his as if for answers. 'Maybe not…'

Gabriel took a step closer. 'Let me show you how it can be, Leo…'

Despite the turmoil in her head and her gut Leonora didn't move when Gabriel took a step closer. Close enough to touch. Her traitorous body craved his. Part of her wanted him to convince her, show her again how he could transport her. Transform her.

He was going to convince her to acquiesce—and, heaven help her, she was going to let him.

Desperately, at the last moment, she tried to assure herself that she wasn't saying *yes* yet. She was just allowing him to…to persuade her. But as his hands cupped her face and his mouth landed on hers she knew she was lying to herself.

She'd already made her decision and it was based on many logical reasons—everything he'd outlined. But it was also based on *illogical* reasons—reasons that had to do with motivations that came from a far more secret place. A place where she harboured dreams that she'd be a fool to believe a man like Gabriel would be able to fulfil.

Dreams of a happy marriage—of an old couple walking hand in hand together after a long life lived in love…

But he was kissing her now, and all those dreams dissolved under his hot touch.

When her legs no longer felt capable of holding her up Gabriel lifted her against his chest and carried her through the vast and echoing *castillo*, with the weight of history all around them, into his bedroom.

He undressed her. Undid her belt and pulled it off. Opened the buttons of her dress and pushed it apart, baring her to his gaze before tugging it over her shoulders and down her arms. Then undid her bra, releasing her breasts to his hands and mouth.

He laid her on his bed and pulled down her panties, pushed apart her legs and tortured her with his mouth until she was gripping the sheets and trembling with the effort it took not to shatter. But of course he wouldn't allow her that mercy, and he pushed her until she came in great shuddering waves, against his mouth.

And then, when she was still pulsating and dizzy from

that shattering peak, he wound her up again, demonstrating the ease with which he could manipulate her. He thrust into her, stealing her breath and robbing her rational mind of any last coherent thought. He wound her higher and higher, until she was thrashing under him, begging, pleading for mercy.

And that was the moment when he stopped and said, 'Look at me, Leo…look at me.'

She forced her blurry vision to take him in, and it was a majestic sight as he reared over her, his body embedded in hers, every muscle straining with the effort it took not to let go. His face was flushed. Eyes burning.

Her whole body was poised on the precipice—one more thrust and she'd be set free. But he wasn't moving. She raised her hips but he pulled back. She scowled at him and he smiled wickedly. She was laid bare. Exposed. Nowhere to hide. And yet she felt a measure of power, the same power she'd experienced the first night they were together. A very feminine power.

Gabriel's body trembled against hers with the effort it was taking him to stop moving, over her, in her, and that gave her some solace.

And then he said, 'What do you want?'

His question got to her, breaking some last vestige of resistance. She suspected he was asking something deeper than just if she wanted release, but her brain was too melted to study it.

'You…' she said brokenly. 'I want you, Gabriel.'

For a moment he still didn't move. And then, just when she was about to beg him to release her from the tension, and from his too intense gaze, he finally moved, and with a broken cry she soared into bliss.

It was raw and visceral and she suspected that she'd just acquiesced to everything he'd asked of her without even saying *yes*.

* * *

The next morning when Leonora woke she felt deeply sated and at peace. It took a long moment for her to figure out where she was and why she was feeling like this. Then it all rushed back.

The proposal.

Making love.

She shivered under the thin sheet. 'Making love' sounded so…so benign, when it had felt more like breaking her apart and putting her back together in a new configuration.

She was alone in the room. She looked around it in the early morning light. It was surprisingly bare—not unlike the bedroom in Gabriel's apartment in the city. Like the man—no frills or flounces or flowery words. Just direct words like *I want you,* or *A proposal of marriage.*

Leonora got out of bed, afraid that Gabriel might appear at any moment and find her feeling so raw. She pulled on a robe that had been laid at the end of the bed—*considerate*—and went into the bathroom.

She looked at herself in the mirror, expecting to see a bedraggled mess. But her eyes were shining and her cheeks still had vestiges of pink in them. She cursed herself. Betrayed by her own body. She paced back and forth, knowing that Gabriel would be expecting an answer when she saw him again.

She sent up silent thanks that he hadn't extracted an answer from her in the throes of passion last night. She would have said anything not to have him stop his particular brand of passionate sorcery.

He made her feel as alive as she'd ever felt and he also made her feel scared. Scared for herself. For her heart. The heart she'd hidden for so long and the heart that longed for more than she'd witnessed growing up.

A little voice popped into her head: *Maybe a family can give you that if Gabriel can't?*

Before she could stop her wayward imagination she saw Gabriel in her mind's eye, returning home from work and scooping a dark-haired child up into his arms, before tugging Leonora close so that he could kiss her.

Leonora caught a glimpse of her reflection again and this time she looked slightly wild-eyed. This was precisely why she should say no to Gabriel. He stirred up too many illicit dreams and fantasies. Fantasies that could never materialise. No matter what she felt when they made love-like the only woman in the world.

And yet…did she have a choice? She had to marry. That was her duty and her responsibility. If it wasn't to Gabriel then it would have to be someone else. Because, no matter what she'd said to him the previous evening, the truth was that she *was* a bride for hire—whether she liked to admit it or not.

Was it so bad that she and Gabriel had this insane chemistry? Wouldn't it help a marriage? At the start at least… It couldn't last. He wouldn't want her like this for ever. But maybe by then they'd have children…

There was a knock on the door and Leonora jumped like a scalded cat. 'Yes?'

A woman's voice. 'Señorita de la Vega? Breakfast is being served downstairs in the dining room.'

Leonora's heart was thumping.

Not Gabriel.

'Thank you. I'll be right down.'

Footsteps went away.

Leonora got herself together and washed, and then went back and dressed in her clothes from yesterday, feeling the sting of shame that everyone would know.

But no one looked at her strangely when she went downstairs. If she passed anyone they just smiled politely, clearly busy with the upkeep of the *castillo*. That reminded her of what Gabriel had said about helping with their *castillo*'s renovations. How could she deny her family that?

She entered the hall and Ernesto appeared.

'Please, Señorita de la Vega, this way.'

Leonora forced a smile, even though inside she was cringing at what Ernesto must think of her. 'Please, call me Leonora.'

He smiled benignly at her as he opened the door into the dining room. She walked in and Gabriel stood up from where he was sitting at the head of the table, dressed in a pristine white shirt, tie and waistcoat, which only emphasised his lean body.

'Good morning.'

She avoided his eye, coming into the room, and wished she'd had more make-up to put on, or tied her hair back. She felt dishevelled. Undone.

'Good morning.'

She sat down and the housekeeper appeared with an array of food.

Leonora smiled at her. 'This looks delicious.'

The woman was pleased. 'Let me know if you want anything else.'

When she was gone Leonora still avoided looking directly at Gabriel.

Until he said, 'Look at me, Leo.'

See? Direct.

She put down the coffee pot and looked at him. All strong lines and that sensual mouth. Those mesmerising eyes. Her lower body spasmed reflexively with the memory of what it had felt like to have his powerful body thrusting in and out of hers.

Dios.

'You're a nice person, Leo.'

She blinked. That wasn't what she'd expected to hear. 'Well, I…thank you.'

'You notice people, acknowledge them.'

Now she was embarrassed. 'So do you,' she said, thinking of his interaction with the boy who had parked his car last night.

'See?' he said as he lowered his coffee cup. 'We're well matched.'

Leonora wanted to look away again, but she couldn't. She felt a sense of fatality wash over her. In all honesty, even though the thought of marrying Gabriel scared her to death, because he made her long for so many things, the thought of walking out of his *castillo* this morning and never seeing him again was nearly more terrifying. Never touching him again? *No.*

Before she could really think it through she blurted out, 'Yes.'

'Yes…to what?'

He arched a brow even as his eyes darkened with something that looked like desire but which she suspected was satisfaction. A part of her wished she could say no, just not give him that satisfaction. Did *anyone* say no to this man? She couldn't blame them.

She took a breath. 'You know what. Yes, I'll marry you.'

Gabriel was surprised at the level of tension he'd been feeling, which suddenly dissipated. He hadn't been sure what Leo would say even after last night.

He reached for her hand and lifted it, leaning forward to press a kiss into her palm. He saw how her eyes flared and an answering rush of desire made his blood hot. He wanted to tug her over onto his lap and crush that soft mouth under his, but he forced the desire down. They would have a lifetime for that. Right at that moment he couldn't imagine a day when he wouldn't want her with this fierce hunger, and surely that had to be a good indication that this union would and could work?

It was time to progress—with this woman by his side.

Not wanting to waste another moment of time, he said, 'Would you object to a private wedding service here in the *castillo*'s chapel at the end of the week?'

CHAPTER SIX

LEONORA'S HEAD WAS still reeling a couple of days after she'd agreed to a private wedding which would take place that very week. She'd protested, of course, but with his particular brand of cool logic Gabriel had asked her what advantage there could possibly be in prolonging the wait.

Gabriel had worn her down all too easily, and in the end she'd agreed—it had been the prospect of securing Matías's future sooner rather than later.

She'd come to Gabriel's office in Madrid this morning, to look over a prenuptial agreement. Cruz y Torres Enterprises was housed in a sleek and modern building made of glass and steel. Everyone looked very serious and efficient. She'd been whisked up with a private escort straight to his massive corner office that had a terrace overlooking the city.

'This is impressive,' she said, walking over to a window.

She could feel Gabriel looking at her and her skin prickled with awareness. They hadn't slept together since the other night.

'It's not bad.'

He came to stand beside her and she glanced at him. 'Not bad…? A slight understatement.'

He turned to face her. 'This will be your world too when we're married.'

Leonora balked a bit at that. Somehow she hadn't fully absorbed that aspect. She would be Señora Cruz y Torres.

Suddenly she felt conscious of her very worn suit. It was designer, but practically vintage at this stage, one she wheeled out when she had to look smart. And she'd wanted to look smart today. Professional. Because essentially this was just a business agreement, right?

It might be for Gabriel, but her thumping heart said something else.

A moment of panic made her turn to him. 'Gabriel, I know you think I'm suitable, but really—'

He put a finger to her mouth, stopping her words. He said, 'You're going to be absolutely fine. Trust me.'

He took his hand away.

Leonora swallowed. 'I just don't want to let you down.'

He shook his head. 'You won't.'

There was a taut moment when she thought he was going to pull her close and kiss her, but then there was a knock on the door and she looked around to see a series of officious-looking men and women enter. She was glad of the interruption. She didn't want Gabriel to see how needy she'd felt just then, for reassurance.

The prenup.

She calmed herself and took a seat at Gabriel's desk, where he'd pulled out a chair. She'd looked over the agreement herself at home, when Gabriel had emailed it to her, and she had no issues with it. It was exceedingly generous, actually, with provisions set out for her family and Matías in the event of their divorce. Essentially, he was promising to look after them for their lifetimes.

After she'd signed the agreement, and the legal staff had left, Leonora put down her pen and looked at Gabriel. She felt ridiculously emotional to think that this man, who really barely knew her, was making such a commitment to her family.

'Thank you—you've been very generous.'

He shrugged. 'Your family will become my family, Leo.'

She shook her head, 'But you haven't even met Matías.'

He paused for a beat and then said, 'So take me to meet him.'

Leonora's heart tripped. 'Now?'

'Why not?' He glanced at his watch. 'I can cancel my afternoon meetings—they're not a priority.'

Leonora put in a call to Matías's school. They had no problem with visitors that afternoon, so after some lunch in Gabriel's office they left the city in one of his sleek cars.

They were walking down the corridor, about to meet Matías in the common room area of his school, when suddenly Leonora stopped and said, 'Wait.'

Gabriel looked at her. 'What is it?'

Leonora was suddenly aware of the magnitude of introducing this man to Matías. 'You need to be gentle with him. He can be nervous with strangers and especially protective of me.'

Something crossed Gabriel's face. 'I have a younger sister. I know that's very different, and Estella doesn't have a learning difficulty, but I do know what it's like to worry...'

Leonora couldn't quite compute that Gabriel Torres was here, reassuring her about her own brother. 'Okay.'

She needn't have worried. Within mere minutes Matías was in thrall to Gabriel in a way she could only sympathise with. Staring at him as if he was a god.

It made Leonora's heart twist, because she'd witnessed so many people over the years shunning her brother because he was different. Gabriel seemed to have no such issue, and was talking to Matías as if he was any other young man of eighteen.

They were having an in-depth conversation about football and it turned out they both supported the same team—much to Matías's ecstatic excitement. When Gabriel offered to take Matías to a match some time, the young man—almost equalling Gabriel in height—launched himself at Gabriel, hugging him tightly.

Leonora immediately tensed, waiting for Gabriel to pull back at this display of affection from a stranger, to extricate himself, look awkward, but he didn't. He just hugged Matías back.

To her shock, instead of feeling reassured, she found that watching Gabriel so at ease with her brother was setting her on edge and bringing up emotions she wasn't sure she wanted to identify.

When they finally left, Leonora sat tensely beside Gabriel in his car.

'What is it?' he asked. 'I would have thought you'd be happy to see that Matías and I get along.'

'He really likes you,' she had to admit.

Gabriel shrugged nonchalantly. 'You say that like it's a bad thing.'

Suddenly she realised what was at the root of her unease. Gabriel was too used to getting his own way, having people fall in slavish devotion at his feet. He'd taken Matías's reaction for granted. She was aware that she was irrationally angry with him about that. But it was as if introducing him to Matías had brought home just how quickly and easily she'd let him upend her life. How quickly she'd let herself fall in with his plans.

She looked at him. 'Matías is vulnerable. If you say you'll take him to a football match he expects that to happen. If he likes you he trusts you implicitly, which makes him even more vulnerable. Once we marry, my responsibility to him doesn't disappear. He's only ever known me as his main carer outside of the school.'

Gabriel shot her a glance. 'Are you sure we're just talking about Matías, here?'

Leonora flushed.

'I have no intention of sidelining anyone once we're married, but the fact is that you will have other responsibilities. You'll be my wife, and I have a hectic schedule at the best of times. And once we have children, they'll obviously take precedence. We'll have as much support as we need, but I don't want to entrust my children entirely to the care of staff, as I and my sister were. And as I suspect you and your brother were, until there were no staff.'

That stunned Leonora slightly. 'You want to be involved in your children's lives?'

For a moment he said nothing. She saw his jaw clench, and then he said, 'My parents all but abandoned me and my sister. Left us to our own devices, sent us to schools as far away from them as possible. I was able to handle it. But Estella…she was more vulnerable. I had no idea how badly she was affected. Because of our age gap, when she was a teenager and home for the holidays I was already working in the business. I missed the signs…'

'The signs of what?'

'Signs that she was falling in with a wrong crowd. People happy to take advantage of her limitless wealth, her name and vulnerability.'

Leonora's chest tightened. 'What happened?'

Gabriel was grim, hands tightly on the wheel. 'I found her passed out at home a few years ago. She was unconscious. Nearly dead. I got her to hospital and into rehab and since then she's been doing really well. But the neglect of our parents was a direct cause of her pain and I'll never forgive myself for not seeing it.'

'You weren't her parent. It wasn't your job.'

He glanced at her, and the look on his face made her shiver. 'No. But I knew she wasn't like me. I won't lie—I don't know the first thing about relating to children—but I know that ours will not be neglected and left to fend for themselves.'

Ours. Their children.

They stopped at traffic lights and he looked at her. 'Unless you have other ideas?'

Leonora was still reeling from what he'd just said. She realised he was waiting for an answer. 'No. I want to be involved. Our upbringing wasn't so dissimilar. Until my father lost everything my parents were absent a lot. It was just me and Matías until he went away to school. I can't imagine having children and letting someone else raise them.'

Some of the harshness in Gabriel's expression softened. 'I know Matías is vulnerable and that he takes everything literally. I've made a commitment to you and he's part of that. All your family are.'

Emotion rose inside Leonora. For the first time in years she felt a weight being lifted off her shoulders. She looked away in case he saw it.

The lights turned green.

A car beeped behind them and Gabriel said, 'Leo, we're not moving till you look at me.'

She swallowed her emotion and turned her head. The car beeped again.

Gabriel was unfazed. 'Do you trust me?'

More cars beeped. But the awful thing was that Leonora didn't need the pressure of the traffic building behind them to tell her that *yes*, she did trust him.

She felt as if she was falling off a cliff edge, with nothing to hold on to. When had she allowed herself to trust him so implicitly? How had that even happened? Had it been just now, when he'd spoken of his sister? Or the moment she'd decided to sleep with him? Or the moment she'd seen him being so kind with Matías?

She nodded.

He said warningly, 'Leo... I need to hear it.'

More cars beeped.

A bubble of euphoria was pushing its way up from her chest and she blurted out, 'Yes! Yes, I do... Now drive! Please!'

They moved off smoothly back into the traffic. Cars were overtaking them, beeping their horns, but Gabriel showed no sign of being bothered. A small wicked smile played around his mouth and Leonora felt a lightness she'd never felt before, with anyone.

'You like causing havoc, don't you?'

He glanced at her and his smile grew more wicked.

'Always.'

Instead of being taken home, though, Leonora found herself being driven into the city centre—specifically to an exclusive shopping street in Salamanca. A place she'd avoided for some time, without the funds to purchase designer clothes.

'Why are we here?' she asked as Gabriel navigated expertly into a small parking space right outside one of the world's most expensive designer shops.

He turned off the engine and faced her. 'I've taken the liberty of organising for you to meet with a stylist. Unless you've already sourced a wedding dress and trousseau?'

Leonora flushed. Of course she hadn't. She'd been in denial, wondering how far her dressmaking skills would get her, cobbling together things from her wardrobe and her mother's.

'You'll be back on the social scene as my wife, and you'll need to maintain a certain...standard.'

Leonora swallowed. Again, that was something that had only hit home in that moment of panic at his offices earlier. Uncomfortably, she said, 'I don't like the idea of you buying me clothes.'

A slightly exasperated look came over Gabriel's face. 'You *would* say that, wouldn't you?'

'What's that supposed to mean? I'm sorry if I'm not making this easy for you by merely acquiescing to your every demand.'

Gabriel snaked out a hand and caught her behind the neck. He tugged her forward gently, so gently that she could easily have resisted, and yet treacherously she didn't want to. She *knew* this was part and parcel of marrying a man like Gabriel—so why was she winding him up? Because she wanted to provoke him?

'As long as you acquiesce to *this* demand we'll have no problems.'

His mouth landed on hers like a hot brand, immediately cauterising her thinking process.

'And Señor Torres said that we need to fit you for a wedding dress, yes?'

Leonora's attention came back to the efficient stylist, who had spent the last two to three hours helping her select more clothes than she thought she'd ever know what to do with. Or wear.

'Yes. I'm getting married this weekend.'

Leonora ignored the way the stylist paled slightly. She recovered herself and said, 'Very good. Please, come with me across the road to our bridal selection and we'll see what we have there. Luckily you'll fit most sample sizes.'

Leonora smiled weakly, following the woman across the road to another exclusive boutique. The stylist looked her up and down critically and Leonora said quickly, 'I don't want anything fussy. It's not that kind of wedding.'

What kind of wedding is it, then? a snarky inner voice prompted.

She ignored it.

The stylist disappeared behind a rack of voluminous dresses and Leonora called out, 'Honestly, the more simple the better. In fact maybe it could just be...'

The words died on her lips when the woman reappeared, holding a long dress under protective covering. 'Let's try this, shall we? And go from there.'

Afterwards, when Leonora was changing back into her clothes, she had to admire the skill of the stylist. They hadn't had to go anywhere after that first, perfect dress. Leonora scowled at that. She didn't want a perfect dress. She wasn't like other wide-eyed brides, believing in love and happy-ever-after. Her marriage was a business trans-action, pure and simple. Gabriel was going to provide a dowry to save her family and she would bear him heirs to continue his line.

So why, when she had stood on the raised dais in the shop and looked in the mirror, had she felt ridiculously emotional?

Was it because she knew it was the perfect dress for a *real* wedding? Because in spite of everything she wished this was a real wedding?

Just because she trusted Gabriel Torres, she'd be a mon-umental fool to hope that trust would become something more substantial. If anything, what he'd told her about his parents only gave her more insight into why he was so self-contained. He'd had to learn from a young age to depend on himself. At no point had he mentioned love, wanting it or needing it.

She was still feeling a little raw when she walked back

into the main area of the wedding boutique, and she wasn't at all prepared to see Gabriel sitting on one of the dusky pink chairs, reading a newspaper. He should have looked ridiculously out of place, but of course he didn't.

He looked up when she emerged, and immediately he frowned, standing up. 'What is it? Did something happen?'

She realised she must be still scowling and she forced a smile. 'Nothing is wrong. Everything is…fine.'

The stylist came out behind her, immediately fawning. 'Señor Torres, what an honour. Is there anything we can get for you?'

He glanced at the stylist, and then back at Leonora, a small smile playing around his mouth, as if he knew exactly the turmoil he caused in her heart and her gut and it amused him. She fought not to scowl again.

The stylist was saying, 'Purchases can be delivered to wherever you like.'

He said, 'Have everything but the wedding dress delivered to my *castillo*. After all, that's where you'll be living from next week—isn't that right, *querida*?'

Leonora felt dizzy at that reminder. But she refused to show it.

She went over and slipped her arm through his. 'Yes, of course it is, *mi amor*.' She wanted to see him as off-balance as she felt.

His jaw clenched, but instead of feeling a sense of satisfaction that she'd got to him, all she felt was an ache near her heart.

He thanked the stylist and then took Leonora's hand in his, entwining his fingers with hers, and led her out of the boutique to the street. She slipped on her sunglasses, wanting some kind of armour against Gabriel.

He stopped outside the shop and looked at her. 'You

weren't lying when you said you didn't like the idea of me buying you clothes.'

Leonora's heart thumped. 'It's not that. I'm very grateful—and I know I have to maintain a certain standard. I've just got used to doing without all the fuss and anxiety about what's fashionable and what's not...'

He made a non-committal sound and then he said, 'There's one more place I need to take you.'

He was walking down the street at a brisk pace before she could ask him where they were going. She saw women doing double-takes—men too, for that matter—as they cut through the shoppers. Leonora felt dowdy in her jeans and plain shirt and suddenly lamented that fact, in spite of her words to Gabriel. Right now she wished she was wearing something more flattering. And her hair was still in a rough bun, after the stylist had asked her to put it up to see how the veil would look.

'Where are we going?' She hoped it wasn't somewhere too public.

'My bank.'

Leonora rolled her eyes behind her glasses. Only someone like Gabriel could actually say *my bank* and literally mean *his* bank. The bank that he owned.

The ornate façade of Banco Torres, one of Spain's oldest financial institutions, used mainly now as an investment bank, rose up before them at the end of the street. And Leonora couldn't help but be intimidated as they went through the revolving door into the hushed exclusivity of the marble foyer. Classical statues were dotted around the space. Huge paintings hung on the walls. Presumably Gabriel's ancestors.

A woman approached them, beautiful and sleek in a dark suit. 'Señor Torres, the item you requested is ready in the vault.'

'Thank you.'

Still holding Leonora's hand, Gabriel led her over to where a uniformed security guard was holding an elevator for them. They got in and it went down to the basement level. They were met there by another sleek employee, male this time. He led them through open steel doors and into a long room filled with security boxes. There was a box on the table, and after unlocking it he left them alone.

Gabriel said, 'This is the family vault.'

Leonora looked around. 'Oh...' *Their* family vault had been cleaned out by her father.

Gabriel let her hand go and went over to the box, opening it up. He lifted out a tray and laid it down in front of Leonora. She sucked in a breath. It was a tray full of sparkling rings. Antique rings. Sapphires, rubies, diamonds.

'These rings have belonged to Cruz y Torres brides down through the generations. But if you don't like any of these we can buy a new one.'

Leonora shook her head faintly. As much at the thought of the unnecessary expense as because one ring in particular had immediately caught her eye. It wasn't as ornate as the others. It was much plainer. And yet it stood out.

It was an emerald cut diamond in a gold setting, with a detail of three smaller diamonds either side of the main stone. Classic and elegant.

Gabriel must have seen where her gaze was resting and he picked it out, holding it up. 'This one?'

She looked at him and nodded reluctantly, feeling like a fraud.

He took her hand and said, 'Let's see if it fits.'

Leonora held her breath as he slid the ring onto her finger. It fitted perfectly. She felt a shiver go down her spine as it sparkled up at her benignly.

'This ring belonged to my great-grandmother, actually.

My father's grandmother. Apparently her marriage to my great-grandfather was a rare love-match. She died at the age of eighty, and he died less than a week later of a broken heart. Or so they say.'

Leonora looked at Gabriel suspiciously but he didn't look mischievous. He looked serious.

He said, 'This isn't a love-match, Leo—you do know that, don't you? We have insane chemistry…but that's just desire. I'm not denying that it's a boon for our marriage, but that's all it is. A boon. The important things are our compatibility and the fact that we come from the same world. We both want a different life for our children. But as for love… It's not something I've ever really hoped for or believed in. Sweet stories about my great-grandparents are just…fairy-tales.'

She pulled her hand back, the ring feeling heavy on her finger now. 'Why did you tell me about them?'

He looked at her far too assessingly. 'Because I think you want more from this marriage. More than I'll ever be prepared to give. And you need to know that now.'

Leonora's insides clenched tight. Was she so transparent? She felt the weight of the ring, the cold of the precious metal against her skin. He wasn't telling her anything she didn't already know, but her treacherous heart was shrinking in her chest at his words. In spite of everything, she had hoped for more.

She forced all emotion out of her voice. 'I know what's expected just as much as you do. I've never been under any illusions about what marriage means for me. Do I need to remind you that if the announcement of my engagement hadn't been so rudely interrupted I would be engaged to Lazaro Sanchez right now?'

His expression darkened. He moved closer. 'Do not mention that man's name again.'

Leonora tipped up her chin. 'I've known you intimately for less than a week—do you really think mere sex would turn my head so much that I'd forget a lifetime's lessons and start believing in fairy-tales?'

Gabriel looked at the woman in front of him. She was wearing a plain button-down shirt. He could see a hint of the lace of her bra. She wore faded jeans. Not a scrap of make-up. Her hair was up in a messy knot. She could pass for a student, and yet she had the innately regal grace that belied her lineage.

She was also the most exquisitely beautiful woman he'd ever seen. And every moment he thought he could read her, or figure her out, she slipped through his fingers like quicksilver.

The ring sparkled on her finger in his peripheral vision and something about that was immensely satisfying. Even though he still felt the spike of irritation at hearing her mention Lazaro Sanchez's name. Just the thought that she might possibly be with that man was enough to make Gabriel reach for her, tugging her into him so their bodies were flush.

'It's not *mere* sex—it happens to be amazing sex,' he said in a low, rough voice, already feeling the inevitable rush of blood to his groin.

Colour tinged her cheeks. 'We can't—not here.' She put her hands on his chest.

Gabriel clenched his jaw. She was right. As much as he'd love to turn her around, pull those provocative jeans down and bury himself inside her, he wasn't about to be the first of his line to desecrate the family vault in such a carnal manner. The fact that this behaviour was also totally out of character was something he didn't want to investigate.

'My apartment is less than five minutes from here.'

Leonora desperately wanted to pull back and say something cool, nonchalant. She still stung inside from his warning not to fall for him. But the sting was melting under the rush of blood to every nerve-ending. And she realised that she'd never felt so alive. Fizzing.

She was not a spontaneous person, and she wouldn't have figured Gabriel to be one either. But she was suddenly filled with an urge to unsettle him as he did her every time he looked at her. So she moved her hands down his chest to his waist and then cupped the growing bulge under his trousers.

Instantly his eyes flared with surprise and he sucked in a breath. 'Witch...you'll pay for this.'

Leonora smiled, even though she knew that every time she savoured a small victory like this she was fooling herself if she thought Gabriel's warning would serve as a deterrent. Nothing could save her from herself.

The thing that struck Gabriel most on the morning of his wedding was the equanimity he felt. He'd always imagined that on his wedding day he'd be suffocating with claustrophobia and chafing at the demise of his freedom.

But he wasn't feeling any of those things. He was feeling impatient.

Leonora was ten minutes late. And, while he knew that was traditional, this was hardly a traditional wedding, with only a handful of guests in the Cruz y Torres family church in the grounds of the *castillo*.

He'd managed to drag his mother back from the tropical luxury outpost where she was conducting her latest affair. His father was beside her, glowering. A parody of a united front.

All the more reason why Gabriel felt sure that Leonora was right for him. They wanted the same things for their children. A more holistic upbringing. They had respect and compatibility and that insane chemistry.

He shifted uncomfortably in his morning suit, recalling his totally out-of-character behaviour the other day—taking her back to his apartment mid-afternoon, where they'd lost themselves in a mutual frenzy of need. He couldn't remember feeling that desperate even when he'd been a hormone-fuelled teenager with his first lover.

Leonora's parents were here too. He'd talked to them the night before, when he'd hosted a dinner here at the *castillo* in order to meet them. He liked them. They'd been humbled by their experience and had paid a price that was disproportionate to what they'd done.

There was movement just beyond the church door and Gabriel tensed, surprised to find himself actually experiencing something that felt like...anxiety. A very unfamiliar sensation.

And then she appeared in the doorway. A graceful silhouette. Long white dress, veil obscuring her face. She was on the arm of Matías, whom she'd nominated to be her attendant. Gabriel's sister had desperately wanted to be here, but she was on a fashion shoot in South America and logistically wouldn't have made it in time.

Music began and they started walking down the aisle. Gabriel's breath stopped when Leonora was revealed more fully. The dress was a plain white column—no frills or flounces or ruffles. Just straight, elegant lines, skimming her perfect figure. Long sleeves and a round neck. And yet even from here he could see how the material clung to every dip and curve.

He forced his eyes off Leonora and acknowledged Matías as they arrived at the front of the church. He shook the young man's hand and then Matías went and stood beside his parents.

Leonora stood before Gabriel, face downbent. He willed her to look up at him. She finally did and he saw the shape of her face, the cheekbones, firm jaw. Lush mouth. Huge eyes.

'You look...stunning.'

The priest coughed and Gabriel turned to face him—but not before he found Leonora's hand and wrapped it in his, as if needing to touch her to make sure she was real.

Most of the wedding ceremony was a blur to Leonora. Gabriel taking her hand had been the only thing keeping her anchored to the spot as the enormity of what she was doing had sunk in when she'd reached the altar. She was committing herself to a man who would never love her. She was setting fire to all those secret hopes and dreams she'd nurtured deep inside her for years.

Somehow all this hadn't occurred to her with Lazaro Sanchez. Because she hadn't cared for him as she cared for Gabriel. That unwelcome realisation had made panic flutter in her chest. But then Gabriel had pulled up the veil obscuring her vision and she'd looked at him. And all she'd been able to see were those dark, fathomless eyes, and her panic had dissipated...

'You may now kiss your bride, Señor Torres.'

It was over.

But it was only beginning.

Gabriel cupped her face and lowered his mouth to hers, so slowly and deliberately that she was quivering all over by the time he made contact. Damn him. He knew exactly how to play her.

The kiss was short, but just as devastating as if he'd pulled her close and taken it all the way to deep and explicit. When she pulled back his eyes were glittering. Until now she'd barely even taken in his steel-grey morning suit or the white cravat. It made his skin look very dark.

He took her hand again and led her back down the aisle. Leonora smiled tremulously at her parents and Matías. He was the reason she'd been late. He'd been confused by all the activity and wondering why Leonora was dressed so strangely, and he'd wanted to know what it meant that she would now be living in this new place and not at home.

Very considerately, Gabriel had arranged for one of Matías's favourite teachers from his school to come to the wedding so she could keep an eye on him.

Leonora sucked in big breaths of fresh air once they were outside. A professional photographer took some pictures and then they were ushered into one of the *castillo*'s dining rooms for the wedding breakfast.

Leonora saw her parents awkwardly conversing with Gabriel's parents, who were looking unbearably aristocratic. As if all this was beneath them.

She had caught Gabriel's mother looking expressly at her midsection at one point, and had realised that she must suspect that Leonora was pregnant. Well, she wasn't. Not when she had the all too familiar cramps to prove it.

Leonora had always suffered from particularly painful periods, but it had never been diagnosed as anything but mild endometriosis. She hadn't even considered that she might be pregnant—Gabriel had used protection every time—but she'd been surprised at the tiny dart of disappointment when her period had arrived as usual just the other day.

Was she really ready for babies? Children? The thought was alternately terrifying and awe-inspiring.

She put a hand to her belly now, as she took a sip of champagne, unconsciously easing the lingering ache of the end of her period.

The wedding breakfast was nearly over, so she was surprised when Gabriel tapped his glass and stood up. He looked down at her and then he said, 'I would like to take this opportunity to welcome Leonora into the family, and also to welcome her parents and her brother Matías.' He looked at her and raised his glass. 'You're the future of this family, Leonora—you and our children.'

He took her hand and kissed it and the dull ache inside her was forgotten. She was curiously touched by his public endorsement of her, and the welcome he'd offered to her family. But she could see that his parents didn't totally approve, and they wasted little time in leaving once the party started to break up.

Gabriel had told Leonora that they would be leaving after the wedding for a short honeymoon—again, not something she would have expected of him, having assumed he'd waste no time in getting back to work.

She knew she should be grateful for this time to get to know him better, but as they set off for the airport later that day she couldn't control the butterflies in her belly at the thought of time alone with her new husband.

CHAPTER SEVEN

PARADISE. THAT WAS the only word Leonora could think of as she took in the sight before her. Gabriel had brought her to a paradise that had only ever existed in her imagination. It had a name of course. Costa Rica. They'd flown into the lush tropical country, bordered on two sides by sparkling oceans, late last night, and had then taken a smaller plane to the west coast, where Gabriel owned a villa.

They'd arrived so late and Leonora had been so exhausted that she'd barely noticed Gabriel taking off her outer clothes and laying her down on the softest surface imaginable. But now she was awake. Or was she still dreaming? She wasn't sure.

She'd woken in a massive four-poster bed, with muslin drapes gently moving in the warm breeze. When she'd pushed them back she'd seen the bedroom—wooden floors, rustic furniture. Then wide open doors leading out to a terrace and a glimpse of what could only be described as heaven.

A robe had been laid across the end of the bed, and Leonora had realised she was in her underwear. The strapless white bra she'd worn under her wedding dress and matching lace panties. Refusing to linger on thinking about Gabriel undressing her, she'd pulled the short robe on, and now she stood on a wooden deck, with an infinity pool in

front of her, overlooking a forest and beyond that the sparkling Pacific Ocean.

'Not a bad view to wake up to, hmm?'

Leonora started and turned around with a hand to her
chest. Gabriel was standing a few feet away, holding a cup
in his hand. His hair was damp and he wore casual board
shorts and nothing else. All she could see was that impressive expanse of hard-muscled chest.

She fought for composure. She was still disconcertingly
in that space between waking and sleeping, and the view
in general was not helping to bring her back to reality. *Either* view.

'It's absolutely stunning.' She turned back to the other
view.

He came and stood beside her. 'Did you sleep well?'

Leonora smiled a little sheepishly. 'Like a baby.'

'Good. You deserve a break…'

Leonora didn't like the little warm glow near her heart
when Gabriel said things like that. It was too…seductive.

She forced a breezy smile. 'I'm fine—why would I need
a break?'

'Because you've been carrying the weight of your family's responsibilities for years.'

She rushed to defend them, but Gabriel put a finger to
her mouth before she could.

'I'm your husband now, Leo. You're not on your own
any more. It's not down to you. It's down to *us*.'

Leonora looked up at him. It would be so easy to lean
on this man. So easy to let him just take her burdens and
anxieties. And it was already happening. Her parents had
told her that he'd already set up a meeting for them to talk
with his assistant with regard to carrying out renovation
work on the *castillo* and hiring staff again. And she knew

their association with the Cruz y Torres family would soon have them accepted back into Spanish society.

Familiar anxiety knotted her belly, though. 'What if my father—?'

Gabriel shook his head. 'He won't. I spoke to him and he's agreed to get counselling to try and figure out why he became addicted to gambling. He's learnt a harsh lesson. I'm sure he won't go down that route again.'

Leonora was shocked that he'd discussed it with her father, who had always turned to obdurate stone when she'd tried to broach the subject of counselling or therapy. Perversely, she felt slightly jealous that he'd made more headway than she or her mother ever had.

As if reading her mind, he said, 'Sometimes it takes a person on the outside to communicate a little more effectively. Your father is ashamed of what he's done.'

Leonora swallowed her defensiveness. She realised that after living her life solely in service to her parents and her brother and their huge unwieldy home it would be a challenge to let someone else into that space.

'Thank you for talking to him. I think he does want to get better.'

'They're all thousands of miles away and being perfectly well looked-after. Forget about them now. Breakfast? Or would you like to work up an appetite first?'

Leonora's heart sped up. 'An appetite?'

He nodded. 'You owe me something.'

'I do?'

He nodded as he put down the cup and reached for the tie on her robe and undid it. 'You owe me a wedding night. But first…let's take a little dip.'

He pushed back the robe and it fell off her shoulders and down to the ground. Leonora blamed her semi-awake state for the fact that she felt so languorous as Gabriel looked her up and down while she stood there in nothing but two flimsy scraps of lace.

As she watched he opened the top button and his shorts dropped to the ground. He was naked, and she took in the magnificence of his naked form as if she'd never seen it before. *Now* she was wide awake. Her body humming with electricity.

'Turn around,' he instructed.

She did, revelling in the warmth of the morning sun and the humid air. He undid the clasp of her bra and it fell away, floating gently on the breeze. He came up behind her and wrapped his arms around her, his mouth searching for and finding the sensitive spot between her neck and shoulder. She shivered in reaction. All that was separating them was that flimsy scrap of lace, and Gabriel's hands were there now, pulling it down over her hips.

Her panties fell to the ground at her feet and she turned around, heart beating so fast she felt light-headed. He stood back and held out a hand. She took it and followed where he led her to the pool.

As they descended the stone steps leading down into the clear cool water, with the backdrop of nothing but lush nature around them, she felt as if they were embarking on something very elemental.

The fact that this was so far removed from what Leonora might have imagined of a marriage was too huge to absorb at that moment. So when Gabriel reached for her she went willingly, wrapping her legs around his narrow waist, her arms around his neck, mouths fusing and passion drowning out all and any disjointed thoughts except for *this* bliss.

Breakfast turned into a very late lunch that day...

A few days later Leonora was dozing on a lounger under an umbrella by the pool. Since that first cataclysmic morning she'd discovered that Gabriel had a discreet, friendly staff, who melted in and out of the villa every day, leaving food and tidying away the evidence of the previous night's passion.

At first she'd been mortified, but now she was ashamed to say she was already used to the sensation of invisible hands keeping her world pristine. It was a novelty after years of hiring only the most minimal help at the *castillo*, because she literally had not been able to do all the work alone.

Their days had fallen into a lazy, sensual pattern. Leonora would wake late, as she was generally only falling into an exhausted sated slumber as dawn was lightening the morning sky, and Gabriel would already be up, taking calls or doing some work in his airy study on the other side of the villa. He would join her for a late lunch, which would invariably end up with them back in bed.

Leonora blushed now under the umbrella. They were insatiable. She'd never known sex could be like this—so all-encompassing.

The previous night he'd been about to automatically don protection when she'd acted on impulse and put a hand on his, stopping him.

He'd looked at her for a long moment and then he'd put the protection aside and lain down beside her. 'Are you sure about this? Are you ready?'

Leonora had looked back at him, and even through the haze of desire she'd known they were crossing a line. She'd nodded and said, 'Yes. I want children with you. I know it's hard work, because I looked after Matías when he was younger, but these are different circumstances.'

Gabriel had put a hand on her belly. 'These are very different circumstances, *querida*. You're not alone any more. Our children will have two parents who want the best for them, who will support them no matter what. You'll be a great mother. You're amazing with your brother and you love your parents...'

Leonora's heart had felt suspiciously full. She'd reached for Gabriel, pulling him over her, opening her legs around him, guiding him into her body. Skin on skin. No barriers. Telling him without words that she wanted all those things too. *And more.*

That was why she'd stayed silent—for fear of what she might say.

She hated to admit it now, and she told herself it had only been because of the unique sensation of not using protection, but making love to him last night had felt almost...spiritual.

She put a hand on her flat belly, imagining a baby already taking root inside her. And then she told herself she was being ridiculous. It wasn't the right time. But it could happen within the next cycle. Soon.

She realised how badly she wanted it now. She wanted to show Gabriel that their family could be different. That there could be love. Her heart clenched. Her fantasy of a fuller, richer life wasn't just a fantasy any more. No matter what he'd said or how much he'd warned her not to build castles in the air. If Gabriel wanted a different life for his children then who was to say he couldn't fall in—?

'Afternoon, sleepyhead.'

Leonora's eyes snapped open behind her shades. Gabriel was standing beside her sun bed, tall and broad. Barechested. She was glad that the oversized glasses hid what had to be the soppy expression on her face.

She snatched her hand off her belly and sat up. 'Afternoon. Did you have much work to catch up on?'

Gabriel sat down on the lounger next to hers and reached for some of the fruit that his housekeeper had left out for

Leonora in a bowl. He shook his head and his mouth tightened almost imperceptibly. 'A phone call about a project with someone from the other side. Intensely irritating but unavoidable.'

'That sounds...unpleasant.'

He dismissed it with a hand. 'It's not important.' He stood up, holding out that same hand. 'Come on, I want to take you somewhere.'

Leonora stood up, conscious of his eyes running down her body in the cutaway swimsuit. She let him take her hand, hating the way her treacherous heart tripped. He instructed her to put on a caftan and shoes, and then he took her around to the front of the villa, where there was a sturdy open-top four-wheel drive with a wicker basket in the back. She threw a sunhat in the back with the basket.

'Come on—jump in.'

Gabriel swung into the driver's seat, his naked torso gleaming. He looked like a buccaneer.

Leonora got in and Gabriel took off down the winding path. She put her head back and looked at the canopy rushing overhead, the sun breaking through every now and then in a bright flash. She felt...free. Unencumbered.

She didn't want to ruin the moment by saying anything so she let Gabriel drive, noticing his powerful hands on the wheel, the way he drove with speed, yet precision. There was a shadow of stubble on his jaw. His hair was messy in the breeze. He looked younger. Less...stern. When she'd seen him across that ballroom on that fateful first night she never would have imagined him in this kind of environment...carefree.

She had a sudden thought and hated herself for it. But she couldn't help asking, as massive trees rushed past the Jeep on either side, 'Have you ever brought anyone else here?'

She almost hoped he hadn't heard, that the breeze whipping past their faces might have snatched her words away, but she saw his hands clench on the wheel, momentarily.

'Have you ever brought anyone else here?'

The words landed straight in Gabriel's gut. No. He hadn't ever brought anyone else here. Because this was his secret private sanctuary, where he could get away from everything and everyone. And yet he hadn't hesitated at the thought of bringing Leo here.

That question from any other woman would have made him feel as if there was a hand around his neck, squeezing slowly. But this was different. *She* was different. Which was why he'd married her, he told himself now. Because she didn't induce that feeling of claustrophobia. The opposite, in fact.

Seeing the shock and awe on her face that first morning had been worth it alone. He was jaded, and the people around him were jaded. Yet Leo, even coming from the same world, was remarkably *un*-jaded.

He took her hand in his, slowing the vehicle as they veered off the road and onto a dirt track that ran deeper into the jungle. He looked at her. 'No, I've never brought anyone else here.'

She couldn't hide the relief on her face, even though she quickly masked it. And then she surprised him.

'Good,' she said. 'Because if I thought this was just some routine you've done a thousand times I think I'd have to kill you. And those other women.'

Gabriel threw his head back and laughed. Leo was grinning and his chest tightened. She was so beautiful. The sun had added a golden glow to her skin. Her hair tumbled over her shoulders, its normally sleek glossiness untamed in loose waves. And he wanted her with a hunger that only seemed to grow the more he had of her.

On that unsettling thought he let her hand go, ostensibly to put both his hands on the wheel in order to control the car on the rougher terrain. But it was also because he'd just realised how far under his skin she'd reached. All the way so that for the first time in his life work wasn't the first thought of his day. Or his last. It was *her*. And then, when he was sated, he thought about work again. As if he needed to take that edge off before he could think clearly.

He'd had to take a phone call with Lazaro Sanchez just now, and Sanchez had goaded him about using Leonora to score points in their rivalry. Just hearing her name on that man's lips had made Gabriel see red, even as his conscience had pricked when he'd recalled being very aware of how it would look to be photographed with her leaving the hotel the night of the failed engagement.

That felt like a long time ago now. He'd never envisaged then, that Leonora would become his wife.

He'd told Sanchez that Leonora was *where she belonged.* And he'd really meant it. He felt a possessiveness that he'd never felt before—for a woman or anything.

Gabriel shoved aside the niggling prickling sensation that felt like exposure. He was on his honeymoon. It was natural and expected to be captivated by one's wife. Possessive.

Leonora gasped out loud as they burst through the thick trees and onto the edge of the most pristine beach she'd ever seen in her life. Gabriel stopped driving and she stood up in the vehicle, scanning left and right. She could see nothing but sea, white sand and the line of trees bordering the beach. It was completely empty. The waves rolled in with a rhythmic *whoosh*.

Gabriel got out, picking up the wicker basket. Leonora

got out too and stuck her sunhat on her head as she walked to the start of the beach. She slipped off her shoes and dug her toes into the soft warm sand.

It was beyond idyllic and there wasn't another human in sight. Just her and this charismatic man who had come into her life only a couple of short weeks ago and comprehensively turned it upside down and transformed her, inside and out.

Impulsively, she pulled off her caftan and threw her hat down on the sand. She started running backwards towards the sea. 'Last one in is a loser!'

Gabriel stood stock-still for a moment and then he put down the basket, kicked off his own shoes and started running after Leonora. She squealed and turned around, but it was no use. Gabriel caught her all too easily and lifted her up, over his shoulder, and carried her into the crashing surf of the glittering Pacific Ocean, dunking her mercilessly under the foaming waves until she begged for mercy.

He pulled her out, laughing and spluttering, and then she saw the intensity on his face, the way his eyes burned. She reached for him, seeking and finding his hot mouth, revelling in his whipcord body as he lifted her against him, wrapping her legs around him.

The waves crashed around them unnoticed as Gabriel pulled her swimsuit below her breasts, feasting on her wet flesh. The stark contrast of his hot mouth against her sea-cold skin made her head fall back…she was in paradise with the most exciting man she'd ever met and she never wanted it to end…

The knowledge that she'd never felt happier than in that moment was bittersweet. Because she knew it wasn't the same for Gabriel. What he was feeling was purely physical, evidenced by the way he couldn't take his hands off her, or she off him. But, weakly, she avoided thinking about that and gave herself up to the moment, like a miser with her gold.

A couple of hours later, after they'd made love under the shade of the trees on the edge of the beach, Leonora sat with her knees tucked up under her chin, her arms around them. She wore her caftan over her naked body while her swim-suit dried on a nearby rock, with Gabriel's shorts beside it. He wore a towel, tied precariously around his narrow waist.

The detritus of a delicious picnic lay around them. Fruit, bread, cheese, cold meats. Ice-cold water and sparkling wine. Of which Leonora had had a little.

The feeling of happiness lingered in her chest. It was unsettling, because she realised now how little she'd ever felt truly happy in her life. She'd always been so worried about her parents and Matías. And before they'd lost everything she'd always been far too reticent to let her emotions free rein.

'What are you thinking about?'

She glanced at Gabriel, who was sitting back, leaning on one elbow, watching her. He popped a piece of pineapple into his mouth. The thought of blurting out exactly what was on her mind made her break out in a sweat.

She shrugged lightly. 'Just about life…'

'Oh, just about *life*? Nothing much, then?' Gabriel mocked her easily.

Leonora smiled. 'I was thinking about how I used the *castillo* to hide away for a long time. I was so shy… I never felt as if I truly belonged in our world. Everyone else seemed so much more confident than I felt.' She looked at him almost accusingly. 'You even noticed it.'

He sat up too. 'Our perception of other people is usually wrong, you know. Some people just manage to put on a more convincing act. I don't think you're that shy, really. You didn't like being the centre of attention that evening in the hotel, but you did it because you felt you had to. For your family.'

Leonora absorbed that. She hadn't thought about it like that before. He was right—she hadn't liked it, but she hadn't been crippled by it. Maybe her shyness had dissipated over the years and she hadn't even noticed. And he was also right that when it came to doing something for her family she didn't hesitate.

Maybe it would be different if she felt she had a role. A reason to get up in front of people.

She looked at Gabriel and said grudgingly, 'You're very observant.'

He arched a brow. 'I'm observant because I have to be. If I can't read people and I don't see what's going on around me I lose my edge. And if I lose my edge I risk losing everything. My father lost his edge and I had to take over. Too many people depend on me. My family legacy depends on me.'

Leonora touched her belly under the caftan. 'And me too.'

He turned to her and she saw the seriousness of his expression. It cleared, and he smiled, but it was wicked.

'Yes. And you too, Señora Torres.'

He lay down again and pulled her with him, so she was sprawled across his chest. Her breasts were flattened against him and he funnelled his hands through her hair, pulling her head down to his.

'About that legacy… I think it still needs work…'

When his hands reached for her caftan, pulling it up and off her body, she helped, throwing it aside. He removed the barrier of the towel between them and she sat astride him and took him deep inside her on a gasp.

Afterwards, when the sun was setting and it was warm on her naked back, where she lay sprawled across Gabriel's bare chest, she knew she was in deep trouble. All the warnings in the world couldn't stop her falling for this man, because she was already deeply and irrevocably in love with him.

A couple of far too short days later they took off from San José airport. Leonora felt nervous at the thought of leaving behind the idyllic bubble they'd inhabited these past few days. Nervous at the thought of going back into the real world with a man who was still an enigma to her in so many ways—in spite of their physical intimacy, and in spite of her getting to know him in a little better.

They'd discovered similar interests in everything from art to books, movies and politics. But she couldn't afford to forget that the very urbane and seductive man she'd come to know hid a ruthless streak. How could he not be ruthless when he'd shouldered such responsibility for so long and when he was so successful? When he had a legacy to continue?

Physically, their obsession with each other didn't seem to be waning. Far from it. They'd been ready to leave for the airport, dressed and packed, and all it had taken was one burning look from Gabriel and they'd been back in the bedroom, on the bed, clothes ripped off in minutes.

Maybe Gabriel was right, Leonora told herself now. Maybe all they needed was this insane chemistry and mutual respect. And a willingness to commit to bringing up their children differently than they had been brought up in order to have a happy life?

But she couldn't shake the hollow feeling inside her that it wouldn't be enough.

In a bid to try and distract herself, she reached for

the pile of newspapers and magazines left out by the plane's staff.

Almost immediately she noticed a picture on the front page of a tabloid magazine. It was Lazaro Sanchez and the red-haired woman who had crashed their engagement party. They were emerging from what looked like a town hall. She was wearing a cream dress and matching jacket, her bright red hair pulled back into a low ponytail, clutching a posy of flowers. He was in a suit and putting out a hand as if to ward off the paparazzi from getting too close. They'd just been married, clearly.

Leonora couldn't remember him ever looking as intense with her as he did in the photo. She could see the faintest outline of the woman's pregnancy bump. So he *was* the father. No wonder he'd married her so quickly. Her name was Skye O'Hara.

Leonora knew she should be feeling *something* at the sight of her recent almost-fiancé marrying another woman, but all she felt was relief. And a kind of terror to think that she might very well have not had that night with Gabriel which had led to their marriage.

'What's that?'

Leonora looked at Gabriel. She handed the magazine across and he took it, taking in the front cover.

He looked back at her, spearing her with those dark eyes. 'Does this bother you?'

She shook her head. 'No...actually, not at all.'

Gabriel crumpled up the magazine and tossed it in a nearby bin. Then he reached for Leonora, undoing her seat belt and tugging her all too easily out of her seat and into his lap. She blushed and looked around, but there were no staff.

'Sanchez's loss is my gain. He's a fool.'

Leonora looked down at Gabriel. There was a tone in his voice that made her want to ask if he knew Lazaro Sanchez personally, but before she could he was pulling her head down and pressing hot kisses along her jaw and neck. Her head fell back and every coherent thought was wiped out as the last, lingering effects of their magical honeymoon were continued in the luxurious bedroom of the private plane.

Almost a week after they'd returned from honeymoon they were having dinner in one of the *castillo*'s less formal dining rooms.

'How are you settling in?' Gabriel asked.

Leonora thought of the way he'd woken her this morning—the way he woke nearly every morning, actually—in a very sensual way that inevitably put her back into a satisfaction-induced coma for a couple of hours while he got up and went to work. She'd never behaved so decadently in her life.

He was watching her closely and she suspected he was even smirking slightly, which helped her not to blush.

Airily, she pretended not to be thinking about sex. 'Fine, thank you. Ernesto has been very kind. He's shown me every part of the *castillo*. Including the vaults where you store the wine that you don't drink and your family portraits.'

Gabriel took a sip of his sparkling water. 'The portraits are scary, aren't they?'

They were. And they were a sober reminder of the sheer weight and extent of Gabriel's family's legacy.

Unconsciously she put a hand to her belly, thinking that it would have to be miracle if she hadn't fallen pregnant on their honeymoon, given that they'd made love every night and every morning. She'd know in about ten days, anyway.

Now she did blush, which she deflected from by asking hurriedly, 'Why don't you drink—is it just because of your father?'

Gabriel put his glass down. 'That, and I don't like the sensation of not having my wits about me. I once got very drunk when I was a teenager and I never wanted to feel like that again.'

She could understand that. Even though she'd never really been drunk herself, she felt as if she lost her wits every time Gabriel looked at her.

Curious, she asked, 'Why did you get drunk?'

He looked as if he didn't want to say anything, but then reluctantly he said, 'My first lover. She was a bit older than me. I was besotted with her. Until I found her in bed with my best friend.'

Leonora felt her insides plummet. 'You were in love... once?'

He made a face. 'Was it love? It was more like an obsession. And even if it was love she merely confirmed for me that it doesn't exist.'

It was a sign, as if she'd needed one, not to look beyond the physical intimacy of their honeymoon.

She changed the subject and forced a neutral tone into her voice. 'I saw Matías today. He's so excited about the football match in a few weeks. Thank you for getting the tickets.'

Gabriel shrugged nonchalantly. 'I have a box at the stadium. He'll be treated like a king.'

Emotion caught in Leonora's chest. Gabriel really had no idea how a casual gesture could mean so much. 'He'll love it.'

Gabriel asked, 'How are renovations coming along at the Flores *castillo*?'

'Really well. They've done so much already. I think my parents have decided to keep doing the tours. They have plans to make them more dynamic—add in wine tastings, overnight stays, that kind of thing. The fact that they'll be able to hire staff makes all the difference. It's given them a new lease of life. Thank you.'

Gabriel inclined his head. 'It's all part of the agreement.'

That dented a little more of the hazy glow surrounding Leonora. Gabriel wasn't doing this out of the goodness of his heart. He was doing it because it was part of their pre-nuptial agreement. Laid out in black and white. Okay, so his relationship with Matías was something he *was* doing out of the goodness of his heart...but she needed to remember that this marriage was very much a transaction for him. Much as it would have been for Lazaro Sanchez.

She was a commodity who had value in her background, her name, and in how she looked and could conduct herself. And she was lucky that Gabriel found her attractive or she wouldn't be here.

His hand came over hers and she felt that all too familiar tingle of electricity. She almost resented it for a second.

'Where did you go just then?' he asked.

She cursed the fact that she couldn't seem to hide her expressions around Gabriel, when for years she'd perfected the art of not showing anyone what was going on inside her.

She forced a smile. 'Nowhere.'

Gabriel lifted his hand off Leonora's. It was disconcerting to feel so attuned to another person. She'd retreated just then, closing herself off right in front of him. He'd immediately wanted to know why. Even though he was more used to people trying to read *him* for his reactions.

It was also disconcerting how quickly he'd adjusted to having Leonora here at the *castillo*. He almost couldn't re-member a time when she hadn't been there. When he arrived home in the evening the first thing he noticed was her light scent. Floral, with musky undertones. Like her—

serene on the surface but full of complexity and fire underneath.

The captivation he'd felt in Costa Rica didn't appear to be diminishing. During a board meeting earlier his mind had wandered all too easily to remembering how he'd woken her that morning. It had started slow and sensuous but had quickly become urgent and explosive.

She was addictive.

He assured himself that this was normal. He just hadn't expected that he would *want* his wife this much. He'd imagined a far more sedate arrangement, if and when he married, with sex turning into a function more than an indulgence. But this was a *good* thing, he assured himself now. He and Leonora had something to build on. A connection that went beyond what most couples in their world had.

Leonora said, 'Your assistant called me today—about a function in Paris at the weekend?'

'Yes. It's a gala in aid of a charity. It's on at the same time as Fashion Week, so it'll be pretty high-profile.'

Leonora immediately felt intimidated. Which was ridiculous. She'd been bred for this sort of thing.

'When do we leave?'

'We'll fly out Saturday afternoon, and come back on Monday. I have some meetings there on Monday morning.' He put his hand over hers again. 'You'll be fine.'

She looked at him. 'I don't want to let you down. I've never been the most gregarious person in a group.'

He shook his head. 'I don't want gregarious. I want you.'

The hazy glow was back. He interlinked their fingers and Leonora felt a pulse throb between her legs. It was as if her body had been made uniquely to respond to his. It was maddening—and utterly thrilling.

He stood up and held out a hand, the look in his eye very explicit. Unmistakable.

Her body reacted predictably, her blood growing hot, moving faster through her veins.

They'd just finished dinner. Leonora usually liked to relax, watching a boxset or reading a book before bed. But that had been before Gabriel had awoken this needy and insatiable side of her. And right then the thought of losing herself to his expert touch was a very enticing prospect. She really didn't want to think about their first official public outing together as a couple.

So she stood up and let him lead her up the stairs and into their bedroom. She tried to feel cynical about it and remind herself that this attention from Gabriel was in part to ensure a quick result for an heir, but when he touched her, or looked at her like he was doing now—as if, like her, he couldn't quite understand this *thing* between them—it was very hard to be cynical. It felt so pure. And raw. And necessary.

CHAPTER EIGHT

'You look beautiful, Leo.'

She tried to feel confident under Gabriel's approving gaze but a million butterflies were fluttering around her belly. No, buzzing. Fluttering was too gentle. She felt as nervous as she had the night of her engagement announcement.

She checked her reflection again. A styling team had come to get her ready and her hair was in a simple chignon. Her dress was a dark royal blue. Floor-length and fitted, it had three-quarter-length sleeves. It was modest at the front, with a high neckline, but it was backless at the back. A more risqué design than she would usually wear but the stylist had insisted.

Gabriel had surprised her with sapphire drop earrings and a matching bracelet and necklace. The jewels glittered against her skin. She knew she looked the part—she just didn't feel it.

She forced her gaze back to her husband's. 'Thank you. So you do.'

And he did. She'd seen him in a tuxedo before, but he still took her breath away. He wore a white bowtie this evening, and the white of the shirt and the tie made him look very dark.

'Shall we? My driver is ready downstairs.'

Leonora took a breath and slipped her arm through his,

hating how much she liked it that he reached for her hand and held it in the lift on the way down. A little extra touch.

They were staying in a hotel not far from where the function was taking place. An exclusive hotel overlooking the Arc de Triomphe. Gabriel had an apartment in Paris, of course, but it was undergoing refurbishment. He'd taken Leonora there earlier to meet with the designer and get her input on the design. Another unexpectedly thoughtful gesture.

They were in the back of his sleek chauffeur-driven luxury car now, her hand still in his. She wanted to be able to pull away, tell him she was fine, but she wasn't. She saw the flashing of the paparazzi cameras in the distance. The sleek line of cars. The beautiful people getting out.

Bizarrely, at that moment she thought of the picture she'd seen on the magazine cover, of Lazaro Sanchez's new wife… Skye?…and of how terrified she'd looked. Leonora felt a spike of empathy for her.

It was time to get out.

Someone had obviously caught a glimpse of Gabriel inside the car and the camera flashes went crazy.

He looked at her. 'Ready?'

She nodded.

'Wait here. I'll get out first and come around and get you.'

He got out and the shouts were deafening.

'Gabriel! Over here!'

'Where's Leonora?'

'We want to see your wife!'

He came to her door and she sucked in a big breath and stuck on a smile—just as he opened the door and the world became one huge bright flash of light.

After about an hour of milling around the thronged ballroom, after the charity auction had taken place, Leonora's smile felt like a rictus grin on her face. Gabriel was deep in conversation with some very serious-looking individuals, and she'd spied some open doors leading out to a terrace that looked blessedly airy and empty.

She caught his attention and motioned that she was taking a little break, and then made her way through the crowd of well-known faces from film and politics. When she reached the doors she stepped outside, relief flooding her to find the space was indeed empty. Nothing but fresh air and the lights of Paris glittering as far as the eye could see.

She ventured further and then stopped suddenly—because there *was* someone else out here. A woman in a strapless black dress. Petite. Very pretty. With bright red hair. Looking at her with big blue eyes. Shocked eyes.

The woman said, *'You.'*

Recognition was swift. It was Skye O'Hara. Lazaro's pregnant wife.

Leonora looked down and saw the small bump. Inexplicably, she felt a spurt of something that felt like jealousy.

She spoke in English. 'Sorry, I didn't realise there was anyone here.'

She turned to leave, but she heard from behind her, *'No. Please, don't go.'*

Leonora stopped. Tension thrummed through her. She turned around again, schooling her expression to be as non-committal as possible.

Skye said, 'I just want to say how sorry I am… I never intended to ruin your engagement like that. I just… I'd tried to get in touch with Lazaro but it was impossible. I sneaked into that room and saw him… I had to let him know.'

The tortured look on her face and the sincerity of her words made Leonora do a double-take. She was used to a different breed of female. Like the ones who had been gossiping in the bathroom the night she'd met Gabriel. Clearly

Skye was not in their league, and something in Leonora relaxed.

'I know. I get that now. You met before he proposed to me.'

'Yes!' The relief was evident on her face and she smiled ruefully. 'I would have hated it if you'd been with him then.'

Leonora moved closer to Skye. 'No, that would not have been nice. But he would not have done that. These men… they have integrity, at least.'

'You mean Lazaro and…?'

'Gabriel—my husband.' Leonora couldn't stop her gaze from dropping again to Skye's pregnant belly. She looked up. 'Congratulations. I wish you all the best in your future with Lazaro.'

Skye put a small pale hand on her belly. She smiled shyly. 'Thank you…' Then she blurted out, 'I felt it move just now…a proper movement.'

The evidence of Skye's pregnancy only drove home the fact that no matter how in tune Leonora might feel with Gabriel, she really only had one function to fulfil as his wife. Bear him an heir. And she was in danger of forgetting it.

Skye must have seen something on her face. She looked anxious. 'I'm sorry—did I say something…?'

Leonora forced a smile. 'No, not at all. I really do wish you all the best in your future with Lazaro and the baby.'

She turned away to leave but Skye reached out and took her hand. 'I'm sorry again…and I wish you all the best too.'

Leonora was surprised at the surge of emotion she felt at the other woman's touch and sincerity. She squeezed Skye's hand and said, 'Thank you,' and turned away before she could notice the moisture springing into her eyes. Crazy. What was wrong with her? She'd never really had a close female friend, but she realised now that if she had, she would have wanted her to be someone like Skye.

She walked back into the room, her eyes searching out her husband. She didn't have to search for long because he was the tallest man in the room. Well, him and the man he was talking to. Lazaro Sanchez. What on earth would he be talking to *him* for?

Suddenly concerned, Leonora made her way over, seeing the tension in Gabriel's body. And in Lazaro's. The grim looks on their faces. This was not a friendly chat. Far from it. They seemed to be locked in some private battle of wills.

She drew closer and they were still oblivious to her. She picked up their conversation.

Lazaro Sanchez was saying, 'Maybe this time you'll be surprised, Gabriel, and maybe the best bid will win—the one that has the good of the city at its heart, not just the insatiable Torres need for domination in all things.'

Gabriel took a step closer to Lazaro, his face etched in stark lines. 'I do remember you, you know. I remember that day when you confronted my father in the street and claimed to be his son. You have a chip on your shoulder, Sanchez, and it's time to get over it and stop telling yourself you've been hard done by.'

Leonora couldn't believe what she'd just heard. The two men obviously knew each other. Had history. The tension between them was palpable.

She took a step into their space, but even then they didn't notice her. She said, 'Hello, Lazaro, it's nice to see you.'

Lazaro Sanchez blinked and seemed to come out of his angry trance. So did Gabriel, and he immediately reached for Leonora, pulling her close with an arm around her waist.

Lazaro echoed what Skye had said. 'Leonora. I'm sorry for what happened. It was never my intention to do anything to hurt or embarrass you.'

She smiled tightly. 'I know. I just met your wife. Congratulations on the baby.'

'Thank you.'

Lazaro looked at Gabriel and Leonora could feel the tension in her husband's body. He was rigid with it. She'd never seen him react like this to anyone else.

'Till next time, Torres.'

Lazaro walked away.

Leonora looked up at Gabriel, who was staring after Lazaro with a hard expression. Almost bitter. She said, 'I didn't realise you knew each other.'

He looked at her, jaw tight. 'I'd prefer it if we didn't but, yes, we do.'

'You've known him since before the night of the engagement party?'

'Yes, for a few years now.'

Leonora felt sick as things slid into place in her mind. 'A few *years*?'

Instinctively she moved out of his embrace and stood apart. 'You know him and you didn't think it worth mentioning?'

'I didn't think it was relevant.'

Confusion and hurt and other emotions were swirling in Leonora's gut now. 'Not *relevant*? I slept with you on the night I was due to announce my engagement to him— the night you seduced me—and you didn't think it was relevant?'

Gabriel looked around and took Leonora's elbow, guiding her over to a corner of the room where a large plant shielded them a little. That only made her feel more incensed.

She pulled away again. 'Why didn't you tell me you knew him?'

'Because he's not someone I think about unless I have to.'

'You don't like him—that much is obvious.'

'No, I don't.'

The implications of this were huge. 'Why were you even at the engagement announcement if you don't like him?'

Gabriel's jaw clenched. 'Because I needed to know what he was up to.'

Leonora shook her head to try and understand. 'You came after me...after the interruption. I thought it was co-incidental...but it wasn't, was it?'

'I came after you because I wanted you. You felt it too that night. And, I was concerned about you.'

But Leonora wasn't hearing him. She was reliving what had happened in slow motion. She looked at him, feeling the blood drain south through her body, leaving her cold all over. 'You seduced me just to get back at him. You seized an opportunity.'

Gabriel shook his head. 'No, I seduced you because I wanted you—for no other reason.'

Leonora was aware of a sharp pain near her heart. 'Are you telling me you weren't in any way aware of the fact that it might get to Lazaro if you were seen with me?'

Gabriel flushed. 'I admit I wasn't *un*aware that it might irritate him if he saw pictures of us together, leaving the hotel. But once we got back to my apartment Lazaro San-chez was the last person on my mind.'

Leonora shook her head. 'You've used me from the very start—like a pawn. Is that why you proposed? Because it was another way to strike at your adversary?'

Leonora backed away from Gabriel. She had to leave before he saw how devastating this knowledge was to her. She turned and fled, apologising as she bumped into peo-ple in her bid to get out of the function room.

She emerged into a corridor and saw an elevator. The doors were closing and she ran, catching it just before they closed all the way. She stepped in, aware of people look-ing at her. Her heart was pounding. She felt wild. Undone.

She'd just been a pawn all along.

She saw Gabriel emerge from the room just as the doors closed. In that moment, when their eyes met for a split sec-ond, she hated him.

She didn't think when she got out on the ground floor. She went straight to the entrance and jumped into the first taxi she saw...

Gabriel cursed loudly and colourfully enough to make peo-ple stop and look at him at the entrance of the grand hotel. He'd just seen a flash of blue dress and bare back disap-pear into a taxi and the car was already merging into the heavy Paris traffic.

He tried calling Leo's phone but it went straight to voice-mail. Gabriel was not unaware of the irony of his wife being pretty much the only woman who had ever consis-tently demonstrated that he wasn't as irresistible as people liked to make out.

He summoned his own car and got into the back, in-structing the driver to go to his hotel. All he could do was hope that she had returned there.

But she hadn't.

He paced up and down, trying her phone again and again. Eventually he gave up. She'd run because she needed space. He couldn't blame her. His conscience stung hard. He *had* gone after her that first night because he'd wanted her, but he'd also seen an opportunity to stick the knife into Sanchez by letting them be photographed leaving the hotel together.

He just hadn't realised how much he would want her. Sanchez had become very much peripheral to everything once he'd slept with Leo and decided to ask her to marry him.

But could he convince her of that?

'Oú allez-vous, madame?'

Leonora looked at the driver and blinked. Where *was* she going? Her instinct had been to get as far away as possible from Gabriel. But she had a limited amount of cash in her clutch bag and she was dressed in an evening gown. Hardly appropriate to roam the streets, even though she felt it would take miles to work off the anger she felt towards Gabriel.

Anger. *And hurt.*

She knew she had no choice but to go back to their hotel, so she gave the address reluctantly. The taxi did a U-turn in the road and went back the way it had come.

She felt sick. Bruised. And, worse, like a monumental fool. From the moment Gabriel had spoken to her he'd relished her strategic importance in scoring points against a rival.

Would he really be so petty?

Leonora ignored the question. Her anger was too fiery for her to try and be rational, to think this through. Lazaro had seen her as a pawn to use to get him accepted in a world closed to him. And Gabriel had seen her as a pawn to use to get back at Lazaro.

She knew she wasn't a helpless victim in all of this, but the revelation tainted every single interaction she'd had with Gabriel since they'd met. How he must have laughed at her the morning after that first night together when he'd realised that she hadn't even given her virginity to Lazaro. Another point scored.

For a moment she thought she might actually be sick, but she managed to control it. The hotel came into view, glittering in the distance. The taxi pulled up outside and Leonora paid the driver and got out.

As she ascended to their room in the elevator she nurtured her anger, feeling as if she needed some kind of armour against Gabriel's inevitable effect on her. When she reached the door she realised she didn't have a key, so she knocked on the heavy wood.

It opened almost immediately. Gabriel filled the doorway, jacket off, tie loose, top button undone. His hair was messy, as if he'd been running a hand through it. He held his mobile phone to his ear and he had the grimmest expression she'd ever seen on his face.

He said curtly, 'She's here. It's fine. Thank you, Marc.'

He stood aside and took his phone down from his ear. Ridiculously, Leonora felt like a rebellious teenager who'd been caught sneaking home from an illicit party. She refused to let Gabriel make her feel as if she was in the wrong, so she tipped her chin up and stalked past him into the suite.

She turned around to face him. He'd followed her and she could see the anger on his face.

'Don't *ever* do that again.'

Leonora was genuinely confused. 'What?'

'Run away and turn your phone off. We had no way of tracking you or following you.'

'We?'

'My security team. The same security team that protects you without you even knowing it. You're a target, Leo, because *I'm* a target.'

To her surprise, although she could still see the anger, she could also see something else. Fear? And Gabriel looked slightly pale. Or was it just a trick of the light?

But his revelation just stoked her anger. She welcomed it. 'Well, if I had *known* that you had a security team I would have been more considerate. And I didn't turn off my phone when I left. It's been off since we arrived at the event.'

Gabriel ran a hand through his hair, mussing it up more. Leonora hated how fascinated she was by this far less urbane incarnation of Gabriel Torres.

Had he really been concerned?

She pushed that notion down, remembering seeing him go toe to toe with Lazaro Sanchez. The bristling tension between the men.

'Look,' he said, before she could say a word, throwing his phone down on a nearby chair, 'I'm sorry I didn't tell you that I knew Sanchez. I didn't realise how it would look. Or how it would make you feel when you discovered we did know each other.'

She asked tautly, 'What is it between you?'

Gabriel stuck his hands in his pockets. 'Ever since he arrived on the scene a few years ago he's made a beeline for me. Shadowing my every move, trying to disrupt deals I'm involved in. We're both currently involved in a bid to redevelop the old Madrid marketplace.'

Leonora had heard about that bid. It was huge. 'I had no idea you were involved in that.'

The hurt she was feeling intensified. While she'd been thinking that she was growing closer to Gabriel, developing an intimacy that might one day extend beyond the bedroom, he had basically told her nothing about his day-to-day life. It was like a slap in the face.

He looked at her. 'I didn't think you'd be interested.'

'I'm your wife. I think I should know what you're involved in.'

Gabriel walked over to the window. He said, 'I've never had to answer to anyone. I've never had to explain myself.' He turned to face her. 'It didn't occur to me to let you know about these things.'

The anger in Leonora diminished slightly. She could appreciate how a lone wolf like Gabriel might find it hard to adjust to being in a relationship.

Still… 'That doesn't excuse you not telling me about Lazaro. It's too much of a coincidence that we ended up in bed together the same night my engagement was meant to be announced.'

Gabriel shook his head. He came closer, but Leonora backed away. He stopped.

'I went there that night because of Sanchez, yes. But as soon as I saw you I got distracted. It became about you, not him.'

Leonora cursed the fluttering in her belly. 'It was about him when you walked me out through the front door of the hotel.'

His mouth tightened. 'I was aware of how it would look, yes. But I was also conscious of wanting to get you out of there, and getting to know you.'

His straightforward honesty deflated her a little. Her heart beat fast as she recalled how she'd felt the pull between them that night. She'd felt guilty, standing next to her fiancé and being mesmerised by another man. And as soon as he'd asked if she wanted his help in leaving she hadn't hesitated.

As if sensing her weakening, Gabriel said, 'I swear to you, from the moment we got to my apartment Sanchez was not in my head or my thoughts or my motivations. I wanted *you*. Do you really think I would have seduced you into my bed just to get back at him?'

Pride oozed from every inch of the man in front of her. But she resisted the urge to let herself weaken too much.

She remembered something. 'You were saying something to Lazaro earlier…about meeting him in a street with your father. What was that?'

Gabriel's jaw clenched. 'He claims to be my half-brother on my father's side.'

Leonora sat down on the seat behind her. 'What?'

'He confronted us in the street years ago. It was my birthday. He accused my father of being *his* father...but then two of my father's men took him away and I never saw him again until a few years ago.'

'So...he *could* be your half-brother?'

'It's quite possible. My father could have sired any number of illegitimate children.' The bitterness was in Gabriel's voice was palpable.

'Who is his mother?'

Gabriel shook his head. 'I don't know...and I don't care.'

But Leonora saw something. A flicker of emotion. And the fact that Lazaro Sanchez could inspire emotion in Gabriel made her feel almost...jealous. Which was crazy. Jealous of a business rival!

'Did you marry me to get back at Lazaro?'

He took a step forward, a fierce look on his face. 'No. I married you because you were the first woman who made me even want to think about it.'

Suddenly she felt weary. She stood up abruptly. 'I'm quite tired now. I think I'll go to bed.'

She turned before he could see the emotion she was feeling. She suspected deep down that Gabriel wouldn't really have gone so far as to seduce her and marry her just to score points, but it still stung.

He called her name just as she reached the door. She stopped reluctantly but didn't turn around.

He said from behind her, 'You were never a pawn. I went to the engagement announcement that night because of Sanchez, yes. But then I saw you, and I wanted you from that moment. I went after you because I wanted you. I seduced you because I wanted you. And I married you because I knew we'd be good together. Because I want you more than I've ever wanted another woman.'

Leonora's heart beat a little faster. Her hand tightened on the door handle. Gabriel had really hurt her this evening. And his power to hurt her only reminded her of how far she'd fallen. She had to protect herself.

She said, 'I'll take the spare room tonight.'

She walked out with her head held high and didn't look back. But it felt like a pyrrhic victory, because every instinct was urging her to go back and seek solace and oblivion in the arms of the man who had hurt her. Ironically, he was the only one who could help her to forget.

Leonora lay awake in the spare bed for a long time. It was the first night since she'd married Gabriel that she'd spent alone. And her body ached for him.

Dammit.

The hurt she'd been feeling had dissipated. She believed Gabriel. And she knew in her heart of hearts that if she was offered the choice of a sterile, emotionless marriage with Lazaro Sanchez over this…this sea of emotions with Gabriel, she would choose Gabriel again.

Something she'd been clinging to—a sense of injury— dissolved. She realised that her reaction would only reveal to Gabriel that she had feelings for him. Why else would she have been so affected? She thought of his anger because she'd disappeared. The expression of what had looked like fear on his face.

Impulsively, she got up from the bed and went outside the bedroom. The suite was dark. Quiet. She hovered uncertainly outside Gabriel's bedroom door, not even sure what she was going to do, but then she heard a sound coming from the living room so she went in that direction.

She found him sitting on the couch, watching a black

and white movie on TV. One of her favourites. A classic. Her heart clenched. He was still wearing his tuxedo trousers and his white shirt was open at the neck by a couple of buttons, revealing the strong column of his throat. Stubble lined his jaw and her skin tingled with awareness.

Then he looked up and saw her. He stared at her for a long moment, almost as if he wasn't sure she was real. She was very aware of her flimsy silk negligée. Then he slowly sat forward and muted the movie.

He put out a hand and Leonora took a breath and moved towards him. He caught her hand and tugged her down onto the couch beside him. Electric heat flooded her body. Instantaneous. Addictive.

She opened her mouth but he put a finger to it, stopping her. He shook his head. And then he said, 'Let me show you how much I want you. *You*, Leo, no one else.'

Weakly she gave herself up to the temptation she'd denied herself earlier, and with every touch and kiss she blocked out the hurt and the fact that she would undoubtedly face more hurt in the future.

When Leonora woke the next morning the sun was up. She was disorientated, and then she realised where she was and remembered the previous evening. She looked around but the room was empty. She was naked and her body ached all over. They'd made love on the couch, like teenagers, and then Gabriel had taken her into the bedroom and they'd made love again. And then again, as dawn had been breaking. Each as insatiable as the other.

Leonora groaned and rolled over, burying her face in the pillow. She didn't recognise this wanton side of herself. In fact she barely recognised herself at all. Her emotions were so raw and all over the place.

The revelation that Gabriel had known Lazaro all along

still had the power to hurt, in spite of his assurances. He wouldn't be human if he hadn't been aware that seducing Leonora might affect Lazaro's pride. But, having met Lazaro's pregnant wife, Leonora figured Lazaro had more important things to consider than hurt pride.

She put a hand on her flat belly. Could she and Gabriel have conceived a child? Last night? She had to be ovulating around now… Her pulse quickened. Even though everything logical told her that they weren't yet ready for the seismic reality of a baby—they were still getting to know one another!—nevertheless she had to admit that she'd felt a pang of jealousy when she'd seen evidence of Skye's pregnancy.

Leonora suddenly imagined Gabriel appearing and finding her dreaming of becoming pregnant with his baby. She scrambled out of the bed and grabbed a robe. She went into the opulent bathroom and took a shower, standing under the hot spray for a long time, relishing the jets of water on her pleasantly aching muscles.

When she soaped herself she saw the signs of Gabriel's lovemaking: stubble rash on the inside of her thighs. She blushed and quickly rinsed off and got out. She roughly dried her hair and pulled on the robe again.

She steeled herself before she left the bedroom, wishing she could feel blasé and nonchalant after a night like the one they'd shared. They were married, hardly illicit lovers, and yet she felt like a jittery teenager.

When she emerged into the living area she saw the dining table was set up for breakfast. A hotel staff member was there, pouring coffee for Gabriel, who stood up when he saw her.

'Good morning. I ordered a selection of everything. I wasn't sure what you'd prefer.'

Leonora smiled at the staff member as she poured her

coffee and then melted discreetly away. She took in the array of food laid out—fresh fruit, yoghurt, pastries, pancakes, bacon, eggs, toast—and to her mortification her stomach rumbled.

She sat down quickly, avoiding Gabriel's eye, putting some fruit pieces in a bowl and helping herself to some yoghurt.

'How are you feeling?'

Gabriel's question seemed innocuous enough and Leonora risked a glance at him, relieved to see him buttering some toast and not looking at her.

'Fine, thank you.'

Tired. She fought not to let the blush inside her rise to the surface when she thought of why she was so tired.

After a moment Gabriel said, 'I thought we'd spend a lazy day just wandering around the city. If you like?'

Leonora's heart thumped. She swallowed her food. 'You don't have to work?'

He shook his head. 'My meetings are tomorrow and everything is set up for them. It's Sunday—who works on Sundays?'

She'd used to. It had usually been quite a busy day for tourists visiting the *castillo*.

Gabriel said, 'You look surprised?'

Leonora felt self-conscious. 'I think I'd just assumed you'd be more of a workaholic.'

Something fleeting crossed his face, but it was gone before she could decipher what it was.

He said, 'I probably would have found an excuse to work today, but now I have a reason not to.'

It was ridiculous that she felt so excited and yet so trepidatious at the prospect of a day in Gabriel's company. Hadn't she spent a honeymoon alone with him for the best part of a week? But that had felt different—out of reality.

It had all been so new. All-consuming. She hadn't been in love with him then.

She hid her trepidation and said lightly, 'Then I'd like that.' She thought of something, 'What if the paparazzi spot us?'

Gabriel was one of their favourite subjects to follow as he was usually so elusive. But there had been plenty of paparazzi outside the hotel yesterday evening so they knew they were there.

Gabriel wiped his mouth with a napkin and stood up. He said with a wicked smile, 'I thought of that and I have a plan...'

CHAPTER NINE

GABRIEL'S PLAN HAD been to order up some casual clothes from the hotel's boutique, and now he and Leonora, dressed in jeans, shirts, light jackets and baseball hats, were ducking out of the hotel via a back entrance.

Leonora's hand was in Gabriel's as he led her around the side of the hotel. She could see the paparazzi waiting at the front, looking bored, checking their watches, and she couldn't help the small giggle rising as they made their escape. She felt as if she was playing truant from school. Giddy. And even giddier at this unexpected side of Gabriel.

To her surprise, he took her to the nearest Métro station saying, 'It's quicker than a taxi—do you mind?'

Leonora grinned up at him. 'Not at all.'

And that was the start of a magical and totally spontaneous day. They travelled around the city totally unnoticed, blending in with the crowds. Well, as discreetly as a six-foot-plus man *could* blend in with the crowds. Gabriel drew plenty of looks, but not necessarily looks of recognition. And if someone did do a double-take Gabriel and Leonora were usually gone before they realised who it was, having slipped down a side street.

Gabriel had left it to her to decide where to go, so they'd started at the Eiffel Tower and then wandered to the museums, going into the Rodin Museum, where his famous sculpture *The Kiss* had suddenly taken on a whole new significance for Leonora.

They'd stopped for delicious coffee and pastries on the Île de la Cité, near Notre-Dame, and now they were wandering through the leafy Jardin du Luxembourg, chatting easily about inconsequential things.

For the first time Leonora was acutely aware of families. Men carrying toddlers on their shoulders. Babies in prams. Her insides clenched. This could be them some day. And she appreciated more than ever Gabriel's desire for their children to have a different kind of upbringing.

On impulse, when they were standing by the lake in the park, Leonora turned to Gabriel and blurted out, 'I want to have a baby with you.'

He looked at her, a slightly nonplussed expression on his face, his firm mouth twitching. 'Well...that's...*good*...'

Leonora cursed her impetuosity. 'I mean, I know we have to have children, for so many reasons, but I actually... *want* to have a child with you.'

Her heart was pounding so fast. She tried to blame it on the coffee they'd just had. But she knew it wasn't the coffee.

Gabriel suddenly looked more serious. He twined his fingers with hers. 'I know,' he said. 'Me too.'

Leonora felt as if something intensely precious and delicate had been strung between them. And then she saw it: the heat in his eyes. The intent. It sparked the fire inside her and within seconds Gabriel was striding out of the park and flagging down a taxi.

He bundled Leonora in and she looked at him, taking the baseball cap off her head, half terrified and half exhilarated at the urgency suddenly beating between them.

'Where are we going?'

But she knew.

He gave directions to the driver to go back to the hotel, which wasn't far. They were there within minutes.

As they got out Leonora said, 'What about the paparazzi?'

But Gabriel just growled as he tugged her out. 'They don't matter.'

Within a short minute they were back in the hotel suite and Leonora's back was against the door, her mouth under Gabriel's and his hands roving over her body, removing her clothes with ruthless efficiency.

By the time they reached the bedroom, with a line of clothes strewn between the bed and the main door, they were naked.

They fell on the bed, limbs entwined. Leonora didn't know where she began and Gabriel ended. She'd never felt so primal in her life. When Gabriel joined their bodies in one cataclysmic thrust Leonora gasped. It was swallowed by Gabriel's mouth as he started to move in and out, taking them higher and higher, until they could go no further. After a taut moment, every muscle straining against the oncoming rush of pleasure, they fell into it, down and down... and Leonora wasn't even aware that she was crying as her emotions overflowed onto her cheeks.

It was early evening when Leonora woke in the bed alone. She realised her face and eyes were a little sticky and touched her cheeks, horror dawning on her as she realised she'd cried tears of pure emotion while making love to Gabriel.

She got up and dived under a steaming shower, as if that might wash away the signs of her weakness. She prayed that he hadn't seen her emotion. The thought of him realising he'd moved her to tears made her scrub herself even harder.

Eventually she got out, and only emerged into the living area once she'd put on some make-up and pulled back her damp hair. She dressed in casual dark trousers and a thin grey long-sleeved top. Clothes not remotely designed to entice.

Gabriel was standing looking out of the window, and for a moment before he heard her she drank in the tall, broad-shouldered magnificence of him. She wanted him. Again. Already. *Always.*

A sense of desperation mixed with panic gripped her and she felt like fleeing, as if she could escape the way he made her feel, but then he turned around and saw her.

She couldn't help the heat rising into her cheeks and was glad of the dusk outside and the low lighting hiding her reaction.

'I didn't want to disturb you,' Gabriel said.

Leonora's self-consciousness was acute. He hadn't wanted to disturb her—in case she started crying again?

She forced a bright smile. 'I'm awake now.'

He looked at his watch. 'I don't know about you, but I'm famished. We can eat here or go out. It's up to you.'

Leonora's relief that he wasn't making any reference to her tears was short-lived when she imagined sharing an intimate meal in this suite while she still felt so raw. And with the bedroom so near.

She said quickly, 'Let's go out.'

In the back of the chauffeur-driven car on the way to the restaurant, Gabriel found that he was ever so slightly piqued that Leonora seemed so eager to venture out to less inti-mate surroundings. Previous lovers would have been only too happy to capitalise on his undivided attention. But then, Leonora wasn't just a lover. She was his wife. And even as a lover...the lovemaking they shared was nothing like any kind he'd experienced before.

When he thought of this afternoon, and how desperate he'd been, his only consolation was that she'd been as hungry as him. He could still feel her nails digging into his buttocks and hear her rough entreaties. *'Please...don't stop...'*

Gabriel shifted in the seat, irritated. He was regressing. He was no more in control of his body now than he had been when he was a lusty teenager. *Por Dios.*

The car pulled to a stop and now Gabriel was the one who relished getting out of the intimate space. He went around and helped Leonora out.

She looked around her. 'Where are we?'

'Montmartre. There's a good place I know up here.'

He took her hand in his—a gesture that came to him as naturally as breathing air. A gesture he would never have allowed with previous lovers. Somehow it felt ridiculously intimate. But they were married, so that changed everything...didn't it?

They turned a corner and a beautiful square opened out before them, lined with trees and restaurants and bars, music drifting out into the warm evening air.

'Oh, this is lovely!'

Gabriel watched Leonora's face as she looked around, a rare kind of pleasure flowing through him at her reaction.

She caught him looking at her and she blushed.

He said, 'You're unbelievable—do you know that, Leo?'

She looked genuinely confused. 'Why?'

'You were born into one of Spain's oldest dynasties and yet you're not a snob, or spoilt—which, notwithstanding your father's fall from grace, you could very well be.'

Leonora wasn't sure how to respond to that, but she took it as a compliment.

Gabriel led her to a restaurant on the other side of the

square. It looked discreetly expensive. The maître d' greeted them effusively and showed them to a table that was artfully screened off from the other diners, while giving them a view of the charming square.

They were seated and had been handed menus when Gabriel said, 'You could very well have sought out a suitable husband at a much younger age. Why didn't you?'

Leonora hadn't been expecting such a direct question. No one had ever asked her that before. But she'd certainly always been aware of people's looks and speculation whenever she'd appeared in public.

She took a breath. 'I think for a long time I was angry with my father for failing us like that. For being...fallible.'

A cynical expression flashed across Gabriel's face. 'I can attest to just how fallible fathers can be.'

'Once it became apparent that I was the only potential saviour of my family I resented it for a long time. I resented the structures that haven't changed much since medieval times. This notion of having to be married off for the good of the family name. I was made very aware of the fact that our—*my*—only real currency was our name and our lineage.'

'If it's any consolation, things weren't much different for me. I alone am responsible for carrying on the illustrious Cruz y Torres name. My sister doesn't bear that responsibility and I wouldn't put it on her.'

Leonora shook her head. 'And you never minded?'

Gabriel picked up an olive and put it in his mouth, chewing for a moment. 'I never said I didn't mind. When I was younger I contemplated running away many times. That day when Lazaro Sanchez confronted my father in the street and said he was his son... I actually felt slightly envious of him—that he wasn't burdened by the family name.'

Leonora looked at Gabriel. 'Maybe that's what's at the

root of your issues with him. The fact that you're a little jealous of him.'

Gabriel leaned forward and took Leonora's hand. He brought it to his mouth and pressed a kiss to the back of it. He said, 'I was jealous of him that night when he announced your engagement.'

Leonora's heartrate picked up. All she could see were Gabriel's intense eyes, the gold flecks giving them a leonine quality.

There was a discreet cough and with a struggle she looked up at the waiter, for a moment feeling dizzy. Forgetting they were in public. Had they even ordered? She couldn't remember...

Gabriel let her hand go. Starters were placed down in front of them. They ate in silence, and Leonora was glad of a moment to absorb what Gabriel had said, and to tell herself that his admission of jealousy didn't mean anything. He had decided he wanted her that night. That was all. He had an ongoing rivalry with Lazaro. That was all.

As if to reinforce that assertion in her head, their conversation didn't stray into personal territory again. But after the main course had been eaten and taken away Gabriel's gaze narrowed on Leonora.

'Did you enjoy today?'

Leonora was immediately rewarded with a flashback to when they'd arrived back at the suite earlier, ravenous for each other. She took a quick sip of wine—anything to cool her insides.

'It was lovely, thank you.'

He leaned forward. 'I want you to feel valued, Leo. You're not just a pawn. We both grew up knowing we bore a responsibility that most people don't. Our privilege isn't something we got to choose. But I'm glad that I bear this responsibility with you. I think we can be happy together.'

A chill breeze skated across Leonora's skin and she shivered slightly. Gabriel's words circled in her head sickeningly. *'I think we can be happy together'*. Lazaro had said almost exactly the same words just before the engagement announcement.

The truth was no matter what Gabriel said, or how many assurances he provided, she *was* just a pawn. But then, as he pointed out, so was he in many ways. They were both pawns. Somehow that didn't give her much comfort.

It was clear now that today hadn't really been born of a spontaneous desire to spend time with her. It had been a calculated move to make her feel valued. Wanted. Desired. Maybe he hadn't planned that explosive interlude back at the hotel, but all that confirmed was that they wanted each other.

Leonora cursed herself for being so sensitive. She had to develop a thicker skin if she was going to survive in Gabriel's world. The fact that she felt a growing intimacy with him beyond the bedroom—worse, a growing friendship—was all just an illusion. Gabriel was looking on her as an investment to nurture.

Leonora pasted on the brightest smile she could. 'I think we can be happy too.'

Gabriel smiled approvingly.

This was her life now and she had to come to terms with it. To want more... Well, that was just foolish.

In a bid to deflect Gabriel's attention, because he saw too much, Leonora said, 'So, tell me about this bid you're involved in...'

Ten days after they'd returned from Paris, Gabriel was at the public bid for the market space. A project he'd been working on for over a year.

For a man who wasn't used to being unsure of outcomes,

he didn't like to admit that the bid might very well go Lazaro Sanchez's way. The man had come up with a decent plan. A plan that Gabriel could grudgingly respect even if he didn't agree with all of it.

But for the first time in his life the prospect of losing to someone else wasn't his main concern. Something else was distracting him and taking precedence over the bid. *Leonora.*

Things had been slightly *off* ever since Paris, and Gabriel couldn't figure it out.

That Sunday they'd spent together had been one of the most enjoyable days Gabriel could remember in a long time. He didn't have close confidantes. He'd always trodden his own path and had learnt very early on not to trust people. Women or business peers. Everyone wanted a piece of him or to best him.

But he trusted Leonora. Enjoyed spending time with her. *Wanted* to spend time with her. He never would have taken a day off like that before. It had been years since he'd taken the Métro or just wandered around a museum.

But when they'd returned to their suite after dinner on the Sunday night she'd been slightly withdrawn. He'd taken a call, and by the time he'd gone to bed she was asleep. The first night they hadn't made love since they were married.

And then, this week, he'd been busy preparing for the bid, and each night when he'd come back to the *castillo* she'd been in bed, asleep. So he'd hardly seen her. Or touched her. He could feel his hunger for her gnawing away inside him and she should be here by his side today, but she wasn't.

She'd been pale this morning—out of sorts. She'd said something about period pains and had assured him she just needed to rest. So he'd left her behind.

He'd found to his surprise that the evidence that she wasn't pregnant had made him feel conflicting things. Because, as much as he knew he had to have children, he was aware that it was too soon. He wanted more time with Leonora. Alone.

And yet they weren't using protection, so if she wasn't pregnant this month the likelihood was that it would happen very soon. Unless they made a decision to wait for a while, which would go against one of the reasons for this marriage: to have heirs. To continue the family legacy.

This revelation was disconcerting and it made him feel off-centre.

There was a movement in his peripheral vision and he saw Lazaro Sanchez walk over to where his wife had just arrived. Her bright red hair was distinctive. And the small bump of her pregnant belly.

He had to concede that she was not the kind of woman he would have expected Sanchez to go for. She looked... *nice*. Kind. She was smiling, and he could see from here that it was genuine. Warm. Leonora had a similar quality but she was more reserved.

Leonora.

He took out his phone and sent her a quick text, asking how she was.

She replied almost instantly.

Feeling okay, thanks. Good luck with the bid. Sorry I'm not there with you. x

To his surprise, that small 'x' impacted him in his gut, taking his breath for a moment.

Someone approached him. 'Señor Torres? It's time.'

Gabriel saw Sanchez moving towards the stage and

knew he couldn't afford to lose focus now. Sanchez was married, having a baby. Gabriel was also married, and even if Leonora wasn't pregnant now, she would be soon.

There was a lot riding on every decision Gabriel made now. His responsibilities and his legacy were growing exponentially and he wasn't going to let anything distract from that. Not now, not ever.

When Gabriel returned home from the public bid he was met by Ernesto, who looked anxious. 'It's Leonora, sir, she hasn't left the bedroom. She tells me she's all right, but I'm concerned.'

Immediately all thoughts of the bid and the brief altercation he'd had with Lazaro Sanchez afterwards left Gabriel's mind. He looked at his watch. It was early evening. That meant she'd been in bed all day with these pains. Surely this was not a usual menstrual problem?

He took the stairs two at a time to their bedroom and opened the door. Leonora was just a shape under the covers and he went over, his gut clenching with concern. She turned over and he could see even before he reached her that she was pale.

He sat down and automatically put a hand to her brow. It was clammy. 'What is it? Is this a regular occurrence?'

She shook her head, dark hair slipping over one shoulder. Her cheekbones stood out starkly. She was clearly in pain.

'Not every month. Some are worse than others. I have a history of bad cramps. They usually pass within a couple of days. How did the bid go?'

He waved a hand, dismissing that and asked, 'Have you ever seen a doctor about this?'

She nodded. 'When I was younger. He told me it was mild endometriosis.'

She tried to sit up and winced, sucking in a breath.

Gabriel made a split-second decision, pulling out his phone.

Leonora heard him, and went even more ashen. When he'd terminated the call she said, 'Hospital really isn't necessary, Gabriel. I just need to take some more painkillers and I'll be feeling much better by morning.'

Gabriel stood up and said tautly, 'We're not debating this, Leo. You need to get checked.'

Leonora was in too much pain to argue with Gabriel, much as she'd have liked to. She couldn't deny that she was a little freaked out herself, because this month her cramps seemed even more acute than normal.

She got out of bed slowly, trying not to show how much of an effort it took. Gabriel found some shoes and laid them by the bed. As she stood up a wave of dizziness hit her.

Immediately Gabriel was scooping her up into his arms and Leonora realised she was too weak to argue. Most likely from not having eaten all day.

She tried to protest, but he was already out of the room and down the stairs, walking into the main hall, saying something to Ernesto, who leapt to attention, opening the passenger door of Gabriel's car.

Gabriel put her in as carefully as if she was made of fine bone china.

She said, 'Really, there's no need for this...' But he didn't listen to her, strapping her in and closing the door.

Leonora kept her mouth shut as Gabriel drove into the city and stopped on the forecourt of a hospital. People were there to greet them and Leonora was embarrassed—until a wave of pain from her abdomen made her grit her teeth.

An orderly appeared at her door with a wheelchair for

her to sit in, and suddenly she was glad that they were there. Because this was definitely not normal any more.

The following few hours became a blur as she underwent a series of tests. There was a lull while they waited for the doctor to return with some results. Wanting to divert her mind from all sorts of scary possibilities, she asked Gabriel about the bid again.

He turned around from where he was standing at the window, hands in his pockets. His tie was pulled loose, the top button of his shirt open, jacket off and thrown on a chair. His hair was mussed because he'd been running a hand through it.

He said, 'We won't know for at least another month. The two bids have gone on public display at City Hall and the public now has a chance to see both sets of plans and to vote for their favourite. Their vote, together with the city councillors, will decide who gets the commission.'

'Was Lazaro there?'

Gabriel's expression darkened. He nodded. 'Yes—and his wife.'

Leonora plucked at the sheet, feeling guilty. 'I'm sorry again that I wasn't there.'

After all, wasn't that her role now? To be by her husband's side to show support? Lazaro's wife might not have the right name or lineage, but she appeared to be fulfilling her brief far better than Leonora was—on every level.

Gabriel shook his head and came and sat on the end of the bed. 'Don't be silly. It really wasn't that important.'

'But you've been working on it for a year and you hate Lazaro.'

Gabriel stood up, hands dug deep in his pockets again. His jaw was tense. 'I don't *hate* Sanchez...but he winds me up like no one else.'

Leonora squinted at him. 'Are you *sure* you're not related?'

Gabriel made a face, but before he could respond the doctor arrived in the room.

He looked at Gabriel. 'You should go home for the night, Señor Torres. I'm afraid we'll have to do more tests in the morning before we'll be able to give you any conclusive results.'

A sense of dread filled Leonora and she forced herself to ask, 'What do you think it is?'

The doctor looked at her, and she could see the gravity of his expression. 'I'm sorry to say, my dear, that your endometriosis is no longer mild, and probably hasn't been for some time. It appears to be extensive and acute. The fact that your symptoms haven't necessarily been severe up until now is atypical. But every woman with this condition is different. We'll know more tomorrow, when we conclude the tests. I'm sorry I can't tell you more right now.'

A week later

A kindly voice came from a great distance. 'How are you feeling, Leonora?'

She knew it wasn't Gabriel. It was too kindly and he called her Leo.

She struggled to open her eyes, feeling the huge effort it took. When she opened them she shut them again quickly. It was too bright. She was aware of pain...dull, down low... in her abdomen.

There was something pressing on her mind—something urgent—but she knew she didn't want to think about it.

She managed to croak out, 'Thirsty...'

Whoever was there held her head up and pressed something to her lips. A straw.

The kind voice said, 'Drink, Leonora, you'll be feeling better soon.'

But she knew she wouldn't be.

Before she could figure out why, she slipped back down into the dark, comforting place.

'How are you feeling, Leo?'

Gabriel. She knew it was him because she'd been feigning sleep since he'd come into the room, like a coward. But she couldn't keep hiding.

She opened her eyes and blinked in the light.

He looked huge, standing at the end of the bed. Worried. There was stubble on his jaw. For a moment emotion threatened to overwhelm her but she pushed it down. She remembered everything now. She had done as soon as she'd woken properly from the anaesthetic, two days ago.

He said, 'The doctor said you can come home today. But there's no rush. As soon as you're feeling up to dressing.'

She opened her mouth. 'We should...we need to talk about—'

Gabriel shook his head. 'Not now, Leo. We can talk about it when you're feeling better.'

Leonora might have laughed if she'd been able to. Right at that moment she couldn't imagine ever feeling better. But she forced herself to push back the covers and swing her legs over the side of the bed.

Immediately Gabriel was there, but she put up a hand, terrified of what his touch would do to her in her emotionally brittle state. 'I'm fine. I'll have a shower and pack. You should go...have a coffee... I'll be ready when you come back.'

He left the room and she let out a shuddering breath. She felt hollow. Aching. A kaleidoscope of images and memories from the past few days came back into her head before she could stop them.

A doctor standing by the bed, saying, *I'm so sorry, Se-*

ñora Torres, but tests have confirmed that your fallopian tubes are beyond saving. The endometriosis has caused too much damage...surgical removal of the fallopian tubes... you'll still have your uterus and ovaries...'

She was infertile. At the age of twenty-four.

Unbeknownst to her, because her symptoms hadn't been severe, the endometriosis had been quietly and devastatingly wreaking havoc on her insides, cruelly targeting her fallopian tubes, rendering them useless. Beyond saving.

She knew she was still in shock. It hadn't sunk in fully. Nor had the ramifications. She hadn't been able to deal with seeing her parents, though she knew they were worried. Too afraid of what she'd see on their faces. Their terror that this might change everything.

Leonora pushed herself up from the bed and walked over to the private bathroom, locking herself inside. Physically, the doctor had said she should be fully recovered within a couple of weeks. Emotionally, however...

She turned on the spray of the shower and stripped off, stepping into the small cubicle. She used the shower head to clean herself, careful to keep the wound dressing dry.

When she was finished she wrapped herself in a towel and washed her face, brushed her teeth, avoiding looking at her face in the mirror. But then she caught her reflection and stopped. Her eyes looked like two huge pools of pain. Her skin was white, stretched taut, her cheekbones standing out starkly.

All of a sudden she couldn't contain it any more. The emotion rose up and came out of her in great, shuddering sobs.

Gabriel came back into the hospital room carrying coffee for Leonora. He stopped when he heard the sobs coming from the bathroom. His blood ran cold. He'd never heard such a raw outpouring of emotion before, and every instinct in him told him to go to her...but he knew she wouldn't welcome it. This was a very private pain, and for the first time in his life he knew what it was to be helpless.

A week later

Leonora was sitting on a chair on the back terrace of the *castillo*. The late-summer early evening still held lots of warmth, but nevertheless Ernesto had insisted on putting a rug over Leonora's legs.

The spectacular grounds of the *castillo* soothed Leonora's ragged emotions, so she'd taken to sitting here every day, while her body healed on the outside. She was still numb on the inside, though. Still trying to compute the catastrophic loss of her fertility. Every time she tried to dwell on it her mind skittered away.

Her parents had come to visit and her mother had been pale. She'd said, '*Por Dios,* Leo...he'll have to divorce you if you can't give him an heir. What will happen to us?'

Leonora's father had taken her mother away after that, telling Leonora not to listen to her. But her mother was right. And it was something Leonora knew she'd have to discuss with Gabriel sooner or later. The fact that she was no longer capable of providing her husband with an heir.

At that moment she heard footsteps and her skin prickled with awareness. Still. Even after what had happened.

Gabriel came into her field of vision, tall and broad. Dressed in a three-piece suit. His long fingers were tugging at his tie, opening it and the top button of his shirt.

'How are you today?'

Leonora nodded. 'Feeling much better, thank you.'

Gabriel sat down on the lounger beside her, his dark

gaze roving over her face. Leonora knew she must look pale and wan.

'The doctor came to see you today?'

She nodded. 'He was here earlier. I'm healing well.'

Physically.

Gabriel nodded. 'That's good.'

Leonora forced herself to look at him. 'We should talk about—'

He held up a hand. 'We're not talking about anything until you're back on your feet. All you need to think about now is recuperating.'

Leonora swallowed her words.

Gabriel stood up. 'Dinner will be ready shortly. I'm just going to take a shower and change and then I'll come back down.'

Leonora watched him walk away, athletic grace in every move he made. She turned her head, eyes stinging suddenly. She pulled her glasses down over her eyes in case anyone saw her emotion.

Dealing with this diagnosis would be massively disrupting to the best of relationships, founded on love, so what hope could they possibly have? Gabriel could delay the conversation for as long as he wanted, but ultimately Leonora knew this spelled the end of their marriage.

CHAPTER TEN

GABRIEL WAS IN his office, staring out of the window, which took in a spectacular view of Madrid. Sunlight bathed the city in a golden glow. But he didn't see any of that. His thoughts were inward.

It had been two weeks now since Leonora's operation, and physically she seemed to be fine. But emotionally...

Gabriel couldn't begin to fathom what she was going through, and the feeling of helplessness he'd felt that day in the hospital when he'd heard her crying was still there.

Helplessness was totally alien to Gabriel. He was used to being able to influence things, events. And yet even he had to concede that this was entirely out of his control.

There was no amount of money he could throw at the situation to make it better. To restore Leonora to full health.

Unsurprisingly, she'd been withdrawn for the past two weeks. She'd been sleeping in one of the guest suites, in spite of Gabriel's insistence that he would move rooms.

He hadn't liked not having her in his bed. Not at all. It made him feel even more helpless as he watched her retreat further and further to some place he couldn't reach.

There was a knock on his door and he turned around, irritated at the interruption. It was his secretary.

'Sorry, I know you don't want to be disturbed...but it's Lazaro Sanchez.'

Literally the last person Gabriel wanted to see right now.

But to his surprise, instead of issuing an immediate rejection, he heard himself say, 'Send him in.'

Sanchez walked in. Familiar tension and something much more ambiguous mixed in Gabriel's gut.

Leonora's words came into his head. *'Are you sure you're not related?'*

He said, 'To what do I owe this pleasure?'

Lazaro walked over to the desk, and as he did so Gabriel noticed that he looked a little less cocky than normal. As if some of the stuffing had been knocked out of him. He almost felt compelled to say something, but then he noticed a padded envelope in Lazaro's hand.

Lazaro put it down on the desk and tapped it lightly. He looked at Gabriel. 'There is all you need in there to prove that we are related. Which we are. Again, I don't want anything from you or your family—simply an acknowledgement that I am of your blood. It's the least I'm due, I think. Also, I've decided to pull out of the bid for the market. I still think my bid was the better one, but it's not my priority any more. And, yes, you're right. A big part of my motivation *was* in going up against you. You're a worthy adversary, Gabriel, but I've lost the appetite for battling with you.'

Lazaro was almost at the door before Gabriel had recovered enough to say, 'What's changed?'

Lazaro turned around and smiled. 'I've just realised what's truly important in life...that's all.'

He walked out before Gabriel could get his wits back together. Very few people surprised him. But Lazaro Sanchez had just blindsided him. Rapidly, Gabriel tried to assess what Lazaro's agenda might be...but he couldn't come up with anything.

He walked over and picked up the padded envelope. Inside was a piece of paper with the information for a doctor who had a sample of Lazaro's DNA in storage. All Gabriel had to do was provide his own sample of DNA for comparison and they would know if they were related.

But Gabriel didn't need to do the test. He knew in his gut what the result would be. He'd known that day in the street, when he'd first seen Lazaro, that the possibility that he was his kin was very real. In fact, on the other side of the animosity that had played out between the two men, there had been a sense of affinity that he'd never wanted to acknowledge.

It was an unsettling revelation.

Gabriel put down the piece of paper and walked back over to the window. He should be feeling triumphant because he was going to be awarded the bid for the market. But he wasn't feeling triumphant. He was feeling deflated. As if something had been taken out of his grasp.

He realised that he'd relished the fight with Lazaro. The chance to prove himself. Because it happened so rarely.

And then an insidious suspicion came into his mind. Had Lazaro found out about Leo's diagnosis, somehow? Was this why he'd gone a step further in his claim to be of Cruz y Torres blood? Because he knew that if Gabriel didn't have an heir, then any child of Lazaro's would therefore have a claim on the Torres inheritance?

Gabriel shook his head. He was being paranoid. There was no way Lazaro could have found out. It was just coincidence...

But, the fact remained that without an heir, the family name would die out. Even if Lazaro *was* his half-brother, he might not want anything to do with the Cruz y Torres name. Especially after the way he'd been treated...

Gabriel thought of how only a couple of weeks ago he'd been almost hoping that Leo wouldn't be pregnant, so they could have more time alone together. Fate was laughing in his face. Because now they had all the time in the world.

* * *

Leonora sensed Gabriel before she saw him, but she kept on reading aloud to Matías, who had come to the *castillo* to visit her. He'd always loved being read to, and she still did it on occasion. It was like a security blanket, and he'd obviously sensed that something wasn't quite right with his big sister. She hadn't told him about her operation, he'd be too upset.

But Matías had spotted Gabriel and he jumped up from the seat they were sharing and went over, throwing his arms around Gabriel's neck. Gabriel looked at her over Matías's shoulder and she could see it in his eyes.

Now he was ready to discuss things with her.

She'd been feeling perfectly well again for a few days now. Apart from the small scar on her abdomen it would be hard to know that anything had happened. But it had. And it had had catastrophic repercussions.

They both had dinner with Matías, and then he was taken back to his school by one of Gabriel's staff.

Gabriel turned to her at the door, from where they'd waved him off. 'Come and have a nightcap on the terrace?'

Leonora's hand gripped the door for a moment, and then she let go and nodded. 'Sure.'

She followed him out to the terrace, peaceful and fragrant with blooming flowers and plants. Candles flickered gently in the light breeze. Leonora sat down in a chair and tucked her legs underneath her. She watched Gabriel pour himself a coffee and then he looked around.

'What would you like?'

'A little port, please.'

He poured some into a delicate glass and brought it over. Amazingly, considering how battered and bruised her insides were, Leonora felt a flicker of response. She took a sip of the sweet alcohol.

Gabriel came over and sat down on a chair at right angles to hers. His shirt was unbuttoned at the top, revealing the strong bronzed column of his throat and a glimpse of curling chest hair. His sleeves were rolled up and the muscles of his arms were a distraction that sent further tendrils of awareness to Leonora's core.

To her surprise he said, 'I had a visit from Lazaro Sanchez today.'

'Oh?'

'He told me he was pulling out of the bid...that he no longer cares about it.'

'That's...strange.'

From what Leonora had learnt about Lazaro during their short and very chaste relationship, he was ruthlessly ambitious. He'd been willing to marry a woman he hardly knew, after all.

As had Gabriel, pointed out a small voice.

'Yes...it is,' Gabriel said, and took a sip of coffee.

They sat in silence for a while, and then Gabriel put his cup down and sat forward.

Leonora tensed. He looked at her and she saw compassion in his eyes.

He said, 'I'm so sorry, Leo, for what's happened to you. If there was some way I could reverse the diagnosis or offer you a solution then I would.'

He stood up and she realised how agitated he was when he ran a hand through his hair. He cursed and walked over to the wall, placing his hands down on it.

Leonora untucked her legs and sat up, putting down the glass. She wasn't sure what to say.

He turned around and there was a bleak expression on his face. 'I've never felt so helpless in my life. And it's not a nice feeling. To know that there was literally nothing I could do. You were at the mercy of the doctors.'

A little of the ice that had been like a block in her chest for two weeks started melting slightly. She hadn't really thought of this impacting on Gabriel, but of course it must have.

'I know...and thank you for wanting to do something. But nothing could have been done.'

He came back over and sat down. 'It's not fair, Leo... I see you with Matías and know that you'd be a wonderful mother. Loving, caring, compassionate...'

Leonora had been trying not to give in to anger after her diagnosis, so hearing Gabriel articulate it for her was like a balm to her jagged edges.

'Thank you.'

But suddenly he was too close. Emotions were threatening to crack her open from the inside out—emotions she'd been clamping down on for fear of what would be unleashed. Like that day in the hospital, when the storm of grief had left her weak and spent.

She stood up and went to take his place at the terrace wall. She looked out at the view for a long moment, as if hoping it might give her strength, and then she turned, wrapping her arms around her midriff.

'This changes everything, Gabriel. I'm not the woman you married. I can't give you what you need. The sooner we file for divorce, the sooner you'll be free to move on.'

Gabriel stood up. 'Divorce?'

Leonora's arms tightened around herself, as if that might help her contain the rising emotion. 'Yes. Of course.'

He shook his head and came over to where she was standing. 'We don't need to divorce.'

'I can't give you what you need. An heir. Heirs. You're the last in your line and I'm infertile.'

He looked at her for a long moment as the word *infer-*

tile hung starkly in the air between them. Then abruptly he turned away to look out over the gardens.

Eventually he said, 'The doctor assured us that all was not lost. We have options—IVF, adoption...'

'An adopted child wouldn't be of your blood. And IVF is a long and arduous process that may never work. I worked with an IVF charity for a while and I saw the devastation it can wreak on couples, families. Even when it works it takes a toll on the strongest of relationships.'

Gabriel's jaw clenched. 'You don't think *we* have a strong relationship?'

Leonora swallowed, thinking of how rocked she'd been by the revelation that Gabriel knew Lazaro. How hurt.

'I think, like you said, we have a lot going for us... But this was one of the fundamental requirements, and I can't deliver.'

He looked at her. 'Do you want to divorce?'

Leonora couldn't escape that dark gaze. *No.* The word beat through her blood. She'd imagined a life with this man; a life beyond anything she had believed she could have with someone like him. But those fragile dreams had died two weeks ago.

'I think it's the only option.' They'd been married for almost three months, the legal requirement for granting divorce.

Gabriel looked away. His jaw was tight. Leonora knew that for a man like him it was difficult to admit defeat. As he'd said himself, he hadn't liked feeling helpless. But they were both helpless here.

He said, 'I have a full social schedule coming up. Now would not be a good time to draw adverse press attention. We will discuss this again when you are feeling stronger. A lot has happened in the past two weeks.'

Leonora desperately wanted to say, *What is there to dis-*

cuss? But she knew she didn't have the energy to deal with that conversation. So maybe he was right.

'Of course. Goodnight, Gabriel.'

Gabriel watched as Leonora walked back into the *castillo*, effortlessly graceful in a long flowing maxi-dress, her hair loose and slightly more unruly than its usual sleek perfection. Her face was bare of make-up but no less hauntingly beautiful.

'Do you want to divorce?'

'I think it's the only option.'

He still felt slightly winded by the punch to his gut at her suggestion of divorce. Not once since her diagnosis had that possibility even entered his head. But evidently it was the first thing she'd thought of.

He had thought they were building a solid basis for a long and enduring marriage. Solid enough to weather this storm.

Gabriel felt disorientated as he took in the full meaning of the fact that Leonora's diagnosis of infertility hadn't impinged upon him in the same way it had her. She'd been looking for the first opportunity to leave this marriage. And he hadn't.

Fool.

All sorts of insidious suspicions came into his mind. Maybe she'd played him from the start? Just looking for a way to save her family and ensure their security before seeking her freedom via divorce? Even if they'd had children? Maybe she'd just told him what he wanted to hear?

He cursed himself. He more than anyone knew they hadn't married for love. They'd married for myriad reasons—one of which, as she'd pointed out, was to procreate. Have heirs. Continue the line. The legacy.

Now that had been ripped away from them. Leaving... what? The reality that chemistry and mutual respect and friendship weren't enough? He'd mentioned the options that the doctor had given them—IVF, adoption... Gabriel didn't know much about IVF, but he knew enough to agree with Leonora. It was a hugely invasive and precarious method of having children, and she would be the one to bear the brunt of the pain and the procedures.

If she wanted out of the marriage she was hardly going to put herself through those procedures.

An emotion Gabriel had never felt before burned down low in his gut. It felt a lot like hurt.

He slammed his hand down on the terrace wall. No woman had the power to hurt Gabriel. She had made a commitment to him and she would honour it.

He wouldn't accept anything less.

It took hours for Leonora to fall asleep that night. The pain in her heart was almost physical. She couldn't believe how far she'd let herself fall for Gabriel. How far she'd let herself dream that even without his love they could have a good life together. She'd imagined that when the desire burned out they'd have a family to care for, to unite them.

She considered the fact that he'd mentioned IVF. Adoption. Maybe she owed it to him to give it a shot? But then maybe he'd only mentioned it because he felt duty-bound?

She thought of the families she'd met through that charity. She knew what a toll it took, and how it caused huge fissures in relationships and families.

Of course it could be successful, and many people went on to have children, but people who underwent IVF ached to have children and had exhausted every other possibility. They did it for love. And that was not what this relationship was about.

Even if she did agree to undergo IVF and they had children, she realised now that it wouldn't be enough for her to have children without Gabriel's love. It would kill her. She wanted the dream.

Gabriel would move on. He would find another suitable wife and have children. Of that she was sure. He deserved that.

He'd never made her any promises. She would do her duty as his wife for the next few weeks and then they would file for divorce. There was no other discussion to be had. Her infertility wouldn't have magically healed itself in a few weeks.

'You must be very proud, Torres, your wife is stunning.'

Gabriel looked at where Leonora was standing a few feet away. She was a vision in a long ballgown with a fitted sleeveless bodice and chiffon skirts falling to the floor. The gown was ice-blue. Her hair was pulled back and long diamond earrings glittered when she moved her head.

She was indeed stunning. Without a doubt the most beautiful woman in the room. She had an effortless kind of beauty that he could see people noticing and envying. What they didn't know was that her beauty wasn't just skin-deep. Or that she hid a very painful and devastating secret.

He glanced at the man beside him. A business acquaintance who was looking at Leonora far too covetously for Gabriel's liking.

He made his excuses and walked over to her, slipping an arm around her waist.

He felt the tension come into her body at his touch and everything inside him rejected it. It was a over a month now since they'd had that conversation about divorce. They'd been existing since then in a kind of sterile civil environment that was driving Gabriel slowly around the bend.

They were still in separate bedrooms—and Gabriel fully respected the space that Leonora had needed since the operation. But sexual frustration was a constant gnawing ache, exacerbated by the fact that she had retreated to some icy, closed-off place that he couldn't seem to reach.

She was always in bed when he came home from work. She busied herself at weekends at her parents *castillo*, helping with renovations and plans for the business. Or she spent time with Matías.

For someone like Gabriel, who had never envisaged marriage being anything but a means to an end, to find himself *missing* his wife was not a welcome revelation.

The closest they got to any kind of intimacy was at moments like this, when they were amongst hundreds of people. And everything in Gabriel rejected it. Rejected her closing herself off and retreating to a place he couldn't reach. Rejected the notion of divorce.

Leonora was holding herself so stiffly she could hardly breathe. Gabriel's arm was around her waist, and the urge to melt into his side, let him take her weight, was almost overwhelming.

The urge to touch him, kiss him...make love to him was even more overwhelming.

But she couldn't.

The only thing keeping her upright and able to function for the past few weeks was the block of ice in her chest. Keeping her emotions in a kind of deep freeze.

Gabriel represented heat and pain. She couldn't go there. Not when the time was approaching when they would file for divorce. Surely in a matter of days. Once that had happened, and she could maintain her distance from him, she would allow herself to breathe again. To feel the pain she knew she was avoiding.

But it was getting harder and harder. And tonight was worse than any other night.

It was as if he knew how tenuous her self-control was. At every opportunity he was touching her—her back, her arm—taking her hand, massaging her neck.

His touch was like a hot brand through her clothes. As if her body was conspiring with him to just melt and give in.

It would be so easy, whispered a little voice.

But she couldn't. She knew Gabriel wanted her. It was in his eyes every time he looked at her. Or maybe that was just her desire projected onto him?

She was going crazy.

After the operation she'd thought she'd never *feel* again. Feel desire. Hope. Sensation. But the human body was a fickle traitor. Her body seemed disinclined to remember those painful days. It was as if normal operations had resumed in spite of Leonora's emotional trauma.

'Are you ready to go?'

Leonora blinked. As much as she dreaded Gabriel's touch, because of what it did to her, she realised now that on some level she craved these fleeting moments for a few hours every week.

She moved out of his embrace and saw how his jaw tightened. 'Yes, I'm ready to go.'

He put a hand on her elbow and led her out through the crowd. She could feel the tension in his body, reminding her of that night when she'd seen him and Lazaro together.

The function this evening had taken place in the same hotel where her engagement to Lazaro had almost been announced. She'd been so distracted that she only really noticed when they walked outside and there was a barrage of flashes and questions from the paparazzi.

'Leonora! Gabriel! Over here!'

And then there was one voice which seemed to be elevated over all the rest.

'Are you pregnant yet, Señora Torres?'

Gabriel bundled her into the car and Leonora was tight-lipped as he sat into the driver's seat beside her. She was desperately trying to stem the hurt blooming inside her.

He was looking at her. She could feel his gaze on her. Concerned.

'Are you okay? I'm sorry about that—they're idiots.'

Leonora looked straight ahead. 'Just drive. Please.'

Her tenuous hold on her emotions was breaking. Like taut wires finally snapping under the pressure.

Leonora wasn't even aware of where they were going until Gabriel pulled into the underground car park of his city centre apartment. A sense of *déjà vu* slammed into her, further diminishing her sense of control. The memories here—

'Why have we come here?' she asked Gabriel.

He turned off the car engine and looked at her. 'I have an early meeting in town in the morning. There's a fully stocked closet here—it's not a problem, is it?'

Leonora shook her head quickly, in case he might see something. 'No, not at all.'

There was a touch of weariness in his tone, 'There's a spare bedroom here too, Leo. Don't worry, I'm not trying to seduce you again.'

He got out.

For some reason his words felt like a slap in the face. Even though she'd been the one putting distance between them.

He opened her door and put out a hand. Leonora recalled that first night, when she'd been afraid to touch him. She'd been right to be afraid. And she was afraid again now. But she couldn't avoid it.

She put her hand into his and let him help her out.

He let her go again almost immediately, and Leonora

curled her fingers over her palm as if to keep the sensation of his skin on hers a little longer. But it wasn't enough.

In the elevator on the way up she could feel the tension pulsing between them. Like a heart. Beating. A live thing. She studiously avoided looking at Gabriel but she could smell him. Sense him. *Imagine him.* Touching her, removing her clothes, devouring her...transporting her to a place where the pain didn't exist.

The bell chimed, signalling the elevator's arrival at the apartment, and Leonora flushed at her wayward mind.

She stepped out and was acutely conscious of Gabriel behind her. His sheer size and bulk.

This was her first time back in the apartment since that night. She stopped at the entrance to the living area, almost as if she could see in her mind's eye how events that night had unfolded, like a movie. He'd seduced her from the moment their eyes had locked that night at the hotel. Even though she had been about to be betrothed to another.

She turned around and saw him yanking at his bowtie, opening the top button of his shirt. Their eyes met and his movements slowed to a stop.

The words *Goodnight, Gabriel* were stuck in Leonora's throat. She'd said them after every other event. Every night. As she'd made her escape. But tonight...she couldn't say them.

Gabriel frowned. 'Leo...?'

She was breaking apart inside. All the ice was melting and flowing into the whirlpool of emotion she'd been holding back.

She struggled to say something. Anything. 'I can't... I don't know...'

He moved towards her, taking her arms in his hands. His touch burned.

'Leo...what is it? What do you want?'

She couldn't speak.

He came closer. 'Shall I tell you what *I* want?'

Weakly, she nodded, needing him to articulate the turmoil inside her.

He said roughly, 'I want *you*, Leo. I want you so much it hurts.'

He lifted a hand and cupped her jaw. It took every ounce of strength she possessed to try and hold firm. Resist. Not to turn her face into his palm and taste his skin.

'But what's the point?' she asked.

He took his hand away from her face. Something flickered in his expression. Hurt?

'Does there need to be a point? I want you and you want me. That hasn't changed.'

After a long moment of silence he stepped back, and immediately she felt bereft.

He said, 'Go to bed, Leo. It's late.'

He was walking around her and into the apartment and suddenly everything in her rejected him moving away from her. Even though she knew she was the one who had caused him to do it.

She turned around. 'Wait...stop.'

He had taken off his jacket and thrown it aside. She could see the powerful muscles of his back through his shirt.

He turned around.

'You're right,' Leonora said. 'There doesn't need to be a point... I want you, Gabriel.'

For a long moment Gabriel said nothing. It looked as if he was wrestling with something. But then he said, 'Are you sure?'

No.

Yes. She wanted him too much and the floodgates had opened. She needed him to set fire to the emotional turmoil inside her so it would be transformed into something other than this...pain.

She nodded.

He held out a hand. 'Come here.'

She walked forward, her eyes never leaving his face, as if he was a port in the storm. He drew her close and after a torturous moment lowered his head and settled his mouth over hers.

She'd expected instant conflagration. But it was far more subtle than that. His kiss was like a benediction. And it soothed her as much as it frustrated her.

She pressed closer, hands finding his shirt, gripping it tightly. Her tongue sought his, and that first contact was like a match being thrown onto dry tinder. The kiss went from gentle to carnal in seconds and Leonora relished it, seized it.

Gabriel pulled back his head, breathing fast. 'You... Is this what you want?'

Leonora nodded jerkily. 'Please don't be gentle with me. Not now.'

He looked at her as if trying to figure her out, but then he took her hand and led her into the bedroom. He undid her hair, letting it fall loose around her shoulders. Then he pulled down the zip at the back of her dress. It fell to the floor in a swathe of silk and chiffon. She kicked off her shoes and stepped out of it and turned around to face Gabriel, lifting her hands to his shirt.

She tried not to think of that first night when he'd brought her to life. It was too cruel when they couldn't create life.

She almost faltered at that point, but Gabriel took her ineffectual hands from his shirt and undid his buttons, opening the shirt and pulling it off. Then his trousers. Everything until he was naked. And her mind was wiped clean of anything but *this*. Perfection.

Her inner muscles clenched with anticipation. It had only been a few weeks but it felt like a lifetime. Suddenly she was the one who wanted to go slow. She reached out and touched him reverently. Trailing her fingertips over his chest, tracing his muscles.

Then he caught her hand and lifted it to his mouth, pressing a kiss to her palm. Her heart ached. She pulled away and lay down on the bed, slipping off her panties. She hadn't been wearing a bra.

He looked at her for such a long moment that she almost begged him to stop. But then he moved towards her, kneeling on the bed between her legs, pushing them apart so he could come down between them, pressing kisses to her inner thighs.

Leonora caught his hair in her hand, lifting his head. He looked at her, sultry and sexy. Her heart broke.

She said, 'No. I want you…now. Please, Gabriel…'

Because in that moment she knew this was it.

The last time.

He moved up between her legs, taking himself in his hand to guide himself into her.

At the last moment she said, 'Wait, let me…'

He took his hand away and she put her hand on him, around his length, savouring the sheer majesty of his body.

She stroked him until he said, 'Leo…'

And then she took him and guided him home. He seated himself inside her, as deep as he could go. And then, with slow and remorseless precision, he moved in and out.

Leonora could feel the storm building, gathering pace inside her. She desperately clung on, wanting to record every tiny second onto her brain so she could take it out and remember what it felt like. But she knew her memory would be cold comfort…

The point came when she couldn't hold back any longer.

With a sob, she let the energy rush through her, incinerating everything in its wake, and waves of pulsing pleasure made a lie of the pain in her heart...

When Gabriel woke at dawn he knew immediately that he was alone in the apartment. A sense of *déjà vu* mocked him. He opened his eyes. He could still smell Leo's scent. He could still feel her nails scoring his back as her body clamped down on his, so tightly that he'd not been able to hold on, falling over the edge and down into an abyss of pleasure so intense he was still wrung out.

He got up and pulled on jeans. As he'd intuited, the apartment was empty. Like last time, he almost had a moment of wondering if he'd imagined it—but, no. There was a note on the table in an envelope.

Gabriel.

He went over and opened it. There was a card inside. A short note.

Dear Gabriel,
I'm so sorry. I can't do this.
Leonora

His first instinct was to leave immediately and find Leo, track her down and make her say that to his face while that sensual satisfaction still lingered in her blood.

He walked over to the window and looked out at the view. A view he'd always taken for granted until Leo had come into his life and made him see things with new eyes. Unjaded eyes.

That unwelcome sense of helplessness was back. He'd broken through the ice last night but now he was being punished for it. He'd known Leo had been fighting some internal battle when they'd arrived back at the apartment. She'd wanted him but hadn't wanted to articulate it. So he'd walked away. And then she'd said, *'I want you.'*

And he'd wanted to resist. Not to give in. To demand if she was just making the most of the arrangement she wanted to be set free from. But there had been something so raw on her face, in her eyes. And his need for her had been too great.

So he hadn't resisted, even though he'd suspected that he would pay the price. And the price was this.

He looked at the note in his hand again and then crumpled it up.

She just needed space. She'd been through a lot. He would give her a few days and then he would go to her and tell her— *Tell her what?* interjected an inner voice.

Gabriel knew what he had to tell her. He'd known for some time now. But he wasn't sure if she wanted to hear it.

A few days later, after no contact with Leonora, who had gone back to her family *castillo*, Gabriel's assistant came in with a package from a courier. Gabriel opened it and took out a sheaf of papers.

Divorce papers from Leonora.

Something snapped inside Gabriel.

Enough.

He pulled out his cell phone and made a call, standing up and walking over to the window as he waited for the person at the other end to pick up.

If he didn't answer—

But he did.

He heard Lazaro Sanchez drawl, 'Gabriel Torres, to what do I owe the pleasure?'

Gabriel took a deep breath. 'Can we meet, please?'

CHAPTER ELEVEN

'AND THIS PART of the *castillo* was built in the twelfth century—'

Leonora was used to gasps of awe at this point, but not gasps that loud, followed by excited whispers.

She turned around to see that a new visitor had joined the group. *Gabriel.* She put a hand on the wall beside her to steady herself. Maybe it was a hallucination.

But then he spoke. 'Sorry I'm late. Please carry on.'

How on earth did he expect her to just 'carry on'? But then she saw the far too innocent look on his face and a far steelier look in his eyes.

The divorce.

Leonora turned around again quickly, struggling to find her way back into the spiel which she could narrate in her sleep in three different languages.

Somehow she managed to conduct the rest of the tour without making eye contact with Gabriel or tripping over her words.

After the small group of visitors had dispersed and left, she faced him reluctantly. 'Did you get the papers?'

'Yes. Can we talk somewhere private?'

No.

She could see he was angry. Leonora led him into one of the reception rooms and he closed the door behind them.

She moved away from him and folded her arms. 'I don't know why you're here. We've discussed divorcing.'

He came into the room, pacing fast. 'No,' he said, 'Actually we didn't discuss it. You brought it up, I asked if you wanted a divorce, and you said you thought it was the best option. I then said we'd discuss it at a later date. Sending me papers is not a discussion, Leo.'

'I left you a note. I thought that made it pretty clear where I stood. I didn't hear from you.'

He arched a brow. 'Oh, so you're taking that as a signal of my acquiescence? I was giving you space, Leo. Space to think things over. Clearly that was a mistake.'

Leonora's heart thumped. It was heaven and hell to see him again. 'Okay, well here's the discussion—I want a divorce.'

'I don't.'

Leonora looked at him. 'That's crazy. We both know that I can't have children and you need heirs.'

'There are options. IVF. Adoption.'

Leonora turned around to face the window, afraid of her emotions. Damn him. Ever since she'd slept with him they'd been impossible to close off.

'I already told you—they're not viable options.'

'I thought you were better than this, Leo.'

She whirled around, hurt. 'I'm just not—'

He cut in. 'Willing to give us a chance?'

'It's not that.'

'What is it, then? I know IVF is a hard process, Leo, but I know you're strong. And I'd be with you every step of the way.' He continued. 'Did our vows mean nothing to you? For better or worse? In sickness and in health?'

Leonora could feel her blood draining south. 'That's not fair.'

'Isn't it?' He moved closer. 'Why don't you want to try, Leo?'

'It's not that I don't want to...'

'Then *why*? Are you just looking for an excuse to get out? Now that your family are provided for?'

She was horrified. *'No.'*

He was a lot closer than she'd realised. His scent wound around her and she fought against his pull. She stepped back. She had to be strong. Gabriel was just doing what he always did—not taking no for answer. Refusing to see Leonora's infertility as something that couldn't be surmounted.

'No, Gabriel—just *no*. Can't you understand that one little word?'

He was grim. 'I can understand it. What I can't understand is why my wife doesn't think our marriage is worth fighting for.'

He turned away as if to leave and his expression was so stony that Leonora couldn't bear it.

She said brokenly, to his departing back, 'I *would* fight for it. I would do everything in my power to give us a family if I thought for one second that you loved me. But I won't put us through a process that might never work for anything less than love. You deserve a family, Gabriel, and you can have that with another wife. Just not with me. I wouldn't survive it. If it worked we'd have a family, yes, but I don't want to bring a child into the world just to act as the glue in our marriage. And if it didn't work you'd resent me—' She broke off and turned away, trying to stem the sobs working their way up her chest and into her throat.

She expected to hear the door closing behind Gabriel as he made his hasty escape now she'd uttered the word *love*, so she wasn't prepared when she felt his hands on her and he swung her around to face him, his eyes more intense that she'd ever seen them.

'What did you just say?'

She hiccupped.

Gabriel took her over to a couch and sat down, pulling her with him. He took her hands in his. 'What did you say, Leo?'

Her vision was blurry. 'I said, I won't do it for anything less than love.'

He gripped her hands tight. 'Are you saying that you love me?'

She debated denying it for a second. But how could she? She'd just exposed herself spectacularly. She nodded.

Gabriel let her hands go and rubbed the tears she'd shed from her cheeks with his thumbs. She couldn't read his expression. It was something she'd never seen before. A kind of emotional nakedness.

He looked at her. 'I love you, Leo.'

At first his words didn't impact, and then they did. She pulled back instinctively, disbelieving. 'You don't. You're just saying that.'

He shook his head. 'I'm not lying. I would never lie to you.'

'But you don't believe in love. You never wanted it.'

'I didn't. Until a dark-haired temptress captivated me and ruined me for any other woman. I think I fell in love with you the moment I saw you that night in the hotel. I've never had such a visceral reaction to anyone. I had to know you, follow you. *Have you.* And the next morning I knew that this was different. I wanted more.'

Leonora looked at him, searching his eyes, his face. Searching out insincerity. But she couldn't see it. She could only see *him*.

'Why didn't you say something?'

'Why didn't you?' he countered.

She flushed. 'I was scared.'

He said, 'I was in denial. I kept thinking my feelings for you were strong just because you were my wife. It was natural. Expected. I only realised what they truly were when you suggested a divorce... I was so angry. I suspected you of marrying me solely to secure your family's fortune. But mostly I was hurt, and I had to acknowledge that you only had the power to hurt me because I'd fallen for you. And then afterwards...when you closed yourself off...'

'I'm sorry... It was too hard. I was afraid of what would spill out if you touched me. I was barely holding it together. But that night... I couldn't not touch you.'

'And then you left.'

She took his hand. 'Because I knew that I wouldn't survive a loveless marriage. That's my weakness.'

He shook his head. 'It's not weak. It was self-preservation. I was the one who was weak. I was prepared to bully you into staying married to me in the hope that if you agreed to try for a family you'd learn to love me.'

Leonora took her hand from his. 'There's a very strong possibility that we won't ever have children, Gabriel, no matter what we try. If that happens...how do you know I'll be enough for you? What will you do about having no heirs?'

Gabriel took her hand back, lacing his fingers with hers. 'You *are* enough for me. If we never have a family but I have you that's all I need. I've met with my board and we've drawn up a document that details what will happen in the event of my having no heirs. The Cruz y Torres name won't die out. It's a brand now, and brands last far longer and far more effectively than mere humans. And I've also been in touch with Lazaro Sanchez.'

Leonora instinctively held tighter to Gabriel's hand. 'And?'

He smiled a rueful smile. 'He *is* my half-brother. I did the DNA test. He wants nothing to do with the family name or any inheritance. It's a point of pride with him. Even when I told him our situation, and that any children he has might be the only heirs to the Cruz y Torres name. We've also teamed up for a bid on the marketplace. We're going to work *together*.'

Leonora shook her head, as if that might help her to understand everything Gabriel had just told her. 'You did all of that…before you knew…?'

'That you loved me? Yes, I did. I'm not as selfless as you. I wasn't prepared to let you walk away. Ever. You're mine.'

Leonora's vision was blurring again.

Gabriel said, 'You haven't actually said it yet.'

'What?' Leonora could hardly speak over the way her heart was expanding in her chest.

'That you love me.'

Leonora moved so that she was straddling Gabriel's lap. She cupped his face with both hands and pressed a kiss to his mouth. The she pulled back. 'I love you, Gabriel Ortega Cruz y Torres. With all my heart. Is that good enough?'

His hands cupped her buttocks and he expertly manoeuvred her so that she was under him on the couch. He smiled down at her and she could see the sheer love and joy in his eyes, on his face.

He said, 'I want for ever, Leo, is that good enough?'

Leonora looked up at him and saw the intensity blazing from his face and in his eyes. But a tendril of doubt and fear made her say, 'What if we don't—?'

But Gabriel cut her off with his mouth. With a kiss. He pulled back. 'For ever, Leo. No matter what. You are all I need. Anything else will be a bonus.'

She looked up at Gabriel. She saw love and commitment in his gaze. It had been there for weeks, but she hadn't wanted to believe in it. She'd shut it out.

She smiled up at him and wound her arms around his neck as tears pricked her eyes. 'For ever it is, then.'

EPILOGUE

Three years later
Lazaro Sanchez Torres's hacienda in Andalusia

'GETTING YOU TO agree to take on the Torres name was the most difficult negotiation I've ever conducted.'

Lazaro grinned at his half-brother and clinked his beer bottle against Gabriel's glass of water. 'You didn't think I was going to make it easy, did you?'

Gabriel smiled back. 'God, no. That would have been far too predictable. All I can say is that I'm glad we're on the same side now. It makes life so much easier.'

A moment passed between them. Deeply felt emotion. And then a baby's gurgle made them both turn back to the tableau in front of them.

Dragged out onto the back lawn of Lazaro's *hacienda* was a couch, overlaid with colourful throws. On the couch sat Lazaro and Skye's almost three-year-old son Max. He was looking very serious, because lying in each of his arms, propped up by cushions either side, was a baby, the two of them blinking contentedly and kicking their arms and legs in the shade under a huge tree. They were three months old.

'Okay, Max, you're doing so well—just another few seconds.'

Leonora chuckled beside Skye, who had become a good

friend. Her sister-in-law was moving around, getting lots of pictures from different angles with her camera.

Leonora said, 'Poor Max looks terrified.'

Skye groaned and stood up. 'He does, doesn't he?'

She was wearing faded loose dungarees and a bright yellow T-shirt that should have clashed with her red hair but didn't. The swell of her second baby was evident under her clothes, at nearly eight months along.

'Max, smile, sweetie! It's okay—you won't drop them. Honestly.'

Tentatively Max smiled, his blond, slightly reddish hair blowing in the breeze. His blue-green eyes were full of pride at his responsibility as the older cousin.

After another few shots Skye straightened up. 'Okay, that should be loads to work with.'

Skye, who had built up a name for herself as a talented portrait artist, was going to do a painting of Max and his baby cousins, Sofia and Pablo.

After Leonora and Gabriel had made the decision to try IVF, it had taken two years and three painful miscarriages before it had worked, on their last attempt. Gabriel hadn't wanted to put Leonora through even another attempt but she'd insisted. And, happily, that last round had brought them a successful pregnancy and the twins, and every time Leonora looked at them her heart was so full of awe and love that she almost couldn't breathe.

An arm snaked around her waist now and she turned to look up at her husband. Her life.

'Okay?' he asked.

She nodded, feeling emotional. She had a family now, and more fulfilment than anything she'd ever imagined or fantasised about. And a love that she knew would last for ever.

'I'm fine. You?'

Gabriel looked at her and she saw all her thoughts and feelings reflected in his eyes.

'I'm fine too. More than fine. I love you, Leo.'

'I love you too.'

She reached up and pressed a kiss to Gabriel's mouth, and he caught the back of her head, not letting her pull away, deepening the kiss.

'Ugh, kissy-kissy.'

They broke apart, laughing at Max's disgusted pronouncement, and went to rescue their babies, taking one each.

Lazaro said, all too innocently, as he scooped up his own son, 'Honestly, I don't know where he gets that from.'

Skye rolled her eyes and came over to her husband putting her arms around his waist. 'He gets it from seeing his mother being kissed by his father on a regular basis.'

'Oh, and you're a passive partner in that, are you? As I recall, this morning…'

Gabriel and Leonora watched as Lazaro and Skye walked back into the *hacienda*, with Max perched on Lazaro's shoulders. Their voices faded and Gabriel tugged Leonora over to the couch. The sun was setting, bathing everything in a golden and red glow.

Leonora's breasts were heavy with milk. Just as she became aware of that Sofia made a mewling sound. She deftly undid her sundress and placed Sofia on her breast. The small baby suckled hungrily, dark eyes gazing up at her mother.

Pablo snuggled against his father's chest, eyes closed. Leonora and Gabriel shared a look and smiled, not needing words to articulate the love flowing through them and their babies…

* * * * *

LET'S TALK

Romance

For exclusive extracts, competitions and special offers, find us online:

- facebook.com/millsandboon
- @millsandboonuk
- @millsandboon

Or get in touch on 0844 844 1351*

For all the latest titles coming soon, visit millsandboon.co.uk/nextmonth

Want even more
ROMANCE?

Join our bookclub today!

'Mills & Boon books, the perfect way to escape for an hour or so.'

Miss W. Dyer

'Excellent service, promptly delivered and very good subscription choices.'

Miss A. Pearson

'You get fantastic special offers and the chance to get books before they hit the shops'

Mrs V. Hall